MW00981403

PRAY FOR LOVE

As if she had not spoken, Lord Bramton continued,

"In the back of my mind I have always realised it would be quite wrong to marry without love – the real love I have certainly *never* felt for any of the women who have tried to flirt with me."

"But how can you be sure that what you feel for me is not just a passing fad? Like something which comes to you after a good dinner."

"Give me your hand, Galina – "

Because it seemed somehow to be a command, she put out her left hand and he took it in both of his.

His fingers closed over it.

She then felt – although she thought that she must be imagining it – another even stranger vibration running through her entire body.

It was a sensation that seemed to become a thrill.

It touched her heart and then her lips.

Lord Bramton did not speak, but just looked at her.

Then unexpectedly he took his hands away.

"Now you understand!"

"I do not!" Galina protested. "How can you do that to me?"

Lord Bramton smiled.

THE BARBARA CARTLAND PINK COLLECTION

Titles in this series

PRAY FOR LOVE

BARBARA CARTLAND

Barbaracartland.com Ltd

Copyright © 2010 by Cartland Promotions
First published on the internet in April 2010
by Barbaracartland.com

ISBN 978-1-906950-15-6

The characters and situations in this book are entirely imaginary and bear no relation to any real person or actual happening.

This book is sold subject to the condition that it shall not, by way of trade or otherwise, be lent, resold, hired out or otherwise circulated without the publisher's prior consent.

No part of this publication may be reproduced or transmitted in any form or by any means, electronically or mechanically, including photocopying, recording or any information storage or retrieval, without the prior permission in writing from the publisher.

Printed and bound in Great Britain by Cle-Print Ltd. of St Ives, Cambridgeshire.

THE BARBARA CARTLAND PINK COLLECTION

Barbara Cartland was the most prolific bestselling author in the history of the world. She was frequently in the Guinness Book of Records for writing more books in a year than any other living author. In fact her most amazing literary feat was when her publishers asked for more Barbara Cartland romances, she doubled her output from 10 books a year to over 20 books a year, when she was 77.

She went on writing continuously at this rate for 20 years and wrote her last book at the age of 97, thus completing 400 books between the ages of 77 and 97.

Her publishers finally could not keep up with this phenomenal output, so at her death she left 160 unpublished manuscripts, something again that no other author has ever achieved.

Now the exciting news is that these 160 original unpublished Barbara Cartland books are already being published and by Barbaracartland.com exclusively on the internet, as the international web is the best possible way of reaching so many Barbara Cartland readers around the world.

The 160 books are published monthly and will be numbered in sequence.

The series is called the Pink Collection as a tribute to Barbara Cartland whose favourite colour was pink and it became very much her trademark over the years.

The Barbara Cartland Pink Collection is published only on the internet. Log on to www.barbaracartland.com to find out how you can purchase the books monthly as they are published, and take out a subscription that will ensure that all subsequent editions are delivered to you by mail order to your home.

NEW

Barbaracartland.com is proud to announce the publication of ten new Audio Books for the first time as CDs. They are favourite Barbara Cartland stories read by well-known actors and actresses and each story extends to 4 or 5 CDs. The Audio Books are as follows:

The Patient Bridegroom	The Passion and the Flower
A Challenge of Hearts	Little White Doves of Love
A Train to Love	The Prince and the Pekinese
The Unbroken Dream	A King in Love
The Cruel Count	A Sign of Love

More Audio Books will be published in the future and the above titles can be purchased by logging on to the website www.barbaracartland.com or please write to the address below.

If you do not have access to a computer, you can write for information about the Barbara Cartland Pink Collection and the Barbara Cartland Audio Books to the following address:

Barbara Cartland.com Ltd., Camfield Place,
Hatfield, Hertfordshire AL9 6JE, United Kingdom.

Telephone: +44 (0)1707 642629
Fax: +44 (0)1707 663041

THE LATE DAME BARBARA CARTLAND

Barbara Cartland who sadly died in May 2000 at the age of nearly 99 was the world's most famous romantic novelist who wrote 723 books in her lifetime with worldwide sales of over 1 billion copies and her books were translated into 36 different languages.

As well as romantic novels, she wrote historical biographies, 6 autobiographies, theatrical plays, books of advice on life, love, vitamins and cookery. She also found time to be a political speaker and television and radio personality.

She wrote her first book at the age of 21 and this was called *Jigsaw*. It became an immediate bestseller and sold 100,000 copies in hardback and was translated into 6 different languages. She wrote continuously throughout her life, writing bestsellers for an astonishing 76 years. Her books have always been immensely popular in the United States, where in 1976 her current books were at numbers 1 & 2 in the B. Dalton bestsellers list, a feat never achieved before or since by any author.

Barbara Cartland became a legend in her own lifetime and will be best remembered for her wonderful romantic novels, so loved by her millions of readers throughout the world.

Her books will always be treasured for their moral message, her pure and innocent heroines, her good looking and dashing heroes and above all her belief that the power of love is more important than anything else in everyone's life.

"God always answers prayers. I have prayed for love all through my life and God has always answered me."

Barbara Cartland

CHAPTER ONE
1875

Lady Galina More walked out into the garden.

It was May and the daffodils were golden under the trees and the shrubs were just coming into blossom.

She breathed in the fresh air thinking how lovely it was and how much she enjoyed being in the country.

She had been in London for the whole of last week being presented at Court and enjoying the balls that took place every night.

But she could not help feeling it was much nicer to be in the country with her horses.

She was hoping that her brother would be joining her soon as it was lonely without him.

When she had returned home last night, he had a dinner party he had been invited to attend.

"I promise I will be with you before luncheon," he said. "But I dare not chuck this dinner without offending an old friend of Papa's who would be very hurt."

"Then, of course, Georgie, you must go to it, but do not throw me over at the last moment or I shall have to go back to London."

"I think that what we both need is a breather in the country," the Earl of Ranmore replied. "London is all right for a little while, but I am beginning to feel stifled."

Galina felt just the same.

She had been brought up in the country and more than anything else she enjoyed riding her brother's superb horses.

It had also been fun that everyone had told her she was 'the success of the Season'.

'I shall have to go back to London very soon,' she thought, 'otherwise some people will be offended if I have to refuse their invitations.'

There was one she really wanted to accept.

She definitely could not refuse the ball to be given by His Royal Highness the Prince of Wales at Marlborough House.

She had always been totally fascinated by hearing, as everyone else had, about the love affairs of the Prince and she longed to meet the beautiful Princess Alexandra who had captivated the hearts of the English public.

Walking across the lawn she was wondering which of her lovely gowns she should wear on that occasion.

She thought actually it would be a good idea to ask Georgie as he always knew what suited her best.

Her brother was undoubtedly a success as well in his own way.

Not only because he was handsome and had come into his father's title three years ago, but also because he was a superb sportsman.

It was pleasing to know that he had some excellent horses in his stable and he had every chance of winning the Gold Cup at Ascot this year.

There was, however, one matter that worried her more than a little.

Having opened up Ranmore House in London and bought expensive gowns to make her the most fashionable of all the *debutantes*, they had spent a great deal of money.

Georgie had no wife and there was only four years between them.

Thus they ran the family estate together and seldom did anything without asking the other if it was the sensible thing to do.

Now as Galina walked into the shrubbery, she was thinking that she must talk to Georgie about money.

They might have to undertake large economies after they had spent the summer in London.

Opening the house had been very expensive as they needed to take on a much larger staff than they employed in the country because they were entertaining so often.

Actually she enjoyed being hostess to her brother.

Although one of their relations stayed in the house as chaperone, she was getting old. She usually preferred to go to bed before dinner or immediately after it.

It certainly made things easier for them to entertain friends of their own age and there were very many guests to invite who had already offered them hospitality.

It was not surprising that they had so many friends.

Their dear father, the seventh Earl, had held many important posts at Court and that meant he had to spend a great deal of his time at Windsor Castle.

"I am only thankful," Georgie had said, "that Queen Victoria thinks me too young to offer me any of the positions Papa held. I would be bored stiff spending my time kow-towing at the Castle. I do believe Her Majesty is very demanding."

"So I have always heard," remarked Galina. "So do enjoy yourself because sooner or later you are bound to be made Master of the Horse, or as Papa ended up, as Master of the Household."

"I would not mind the first one, but God deliver me from the second!" exclaimed Georgie.

"You are not likely to be either until you marry. I have always heard the Queen insists on the main posts in her Court being held by married men."

"That is because she thinks they will not get into so much trouble as the single ones, but I can assure you that if it comes to *affaires-de-coeur*, the married men are usually worse than the bachelors!"

Galina had laughed, but she thought it was a good thing that her brother was still too young to be shut up in Windsor Castle.

She had only been in London a short time and yet she was well aware that there was usually a sigh on the lips of older gentlemen when they remarked,

"I am so sorry I cannot come to luncheon tomorrow because I am on duty at Windsor."

'Thank goodness,' Galina said to herself, 'Georgie and I are too young to be of any interest to Her Majesty.'

However, she realised that there were a number of important balls she must attend, especially in Ascot Week.

She hoped that she would still be the same success as she had been already.

They were planning to hold a special party for the Royal Ascot races in the box Georgie had reserved. There would be a good number of their guests staying with them as well at Ranmore House in Park Lane.

All of which would cost a great deal of money.

It was something that they could not really afford.

It was Georgie who had insisted on doing things in exactly the same style as his father before him and he had told his sister,

"You are only a *debutante* once in your life, Galina, and you either make a big splash and everyone is aware of you or else you are a failure. No one cares if you are never seen again after the Season is finished."

There was actually no chance of her being anything but a success.

Her mother had been beautiful and Galina was very beautiful too.

She was small with a tiny waist and exceptionally fine legs when anyone saw them. Her hair was the colour of daffodils and her eyes the blue of the sky.

Yet, surprisingly, she did not look so obviously an English beauty as she might have done.

There was something very different about her heart-shaped face and her exquisite Grecian features.

Every man who looked at her looked again.

It was not surprising after being such a success in London that she had received no less than five proposals of marriage.

She thought this was funny and laughed about it to Georgie.

"As though I would accept any man after meeting him only once! I think they must be crazy."

Her brother had smiled.

"You must not forgot, Galina, that you come from a very old and revered family and in addition, my dear sister, they think you are rich."

"*Rich*!" Galina had exclaimed. "How can they?"

"Quite easily, because Ranmore House is one of the largest homes in London, and Ranmore Park is one of the most admired ancestral houses in the whole country."

"But they are not mine, they are yours."

"They make an impressive background for a pretty young lady. And let me say, I admire my sister very much and am very proud of her."

Galina kissed him.

"I would rather have your compliments than anyone else's, and proposals or no proposals, I am looking forward to going down to the country as I would much rather talk to our horses than those stupid young men!"

Georgie had agreed with her.

She knew he was looking forward to coming down today and they had planned a long ride tomorrow round the whole estate.

She walked back to the house and then she realised that it was luncheon time.

She walked into the enormous dining room that was really more of a banqueting hall.

There was a minstrel gallery at one end of the room and Galina could well remember when she was a child the musicians playing there on important occasions.

There was a large ballroom at the other end of the house, but the children's parties had been held in the dining room because it was smaller.

Now, as she sat alone at the top of the table, which was decorated with flowers and fine George II silver, she hoped that Georgie would not be delayed.

'There are very many issues,' she thought, 'I must talk to him about. I know we must think seriously of how much we are currently spending.'

She was waited on by the butler and two footmen and that meant another four were waiting in the hall in case her brother arrived earlier than expected.

She was just sipping her coffee when there was the sound of horses' hooves and wheels.

The butler called out,

"That'll be his Lordship!"

Galina sprang to her feet and reached it just as her brother came through the front door.

"You are back, Georgie, and I was so hoping you would not be late!"

She flung her arms round his neck and kissed him.

"I broke all records with this new team," he said, "they are really excellent and the best I have ever driven."

"Are they the horses you had bought at Tattersall's a week or so ago?"

He nodded.

"You must come and look at them later. They are all perfectly matched and it must have broken Fitzhaven's heart to part with them."

As he was speaking, the Earl was handing his hat and coat to the footmen.

He smoothed back his hair and walked towards the dining room with Galina beside him.

"Why did he have to part with these horses?"

"For the obvious reason! He is hard up and had to sell them."

Galina was silent.

She was thinking of the horses they both loved and how terrible it would be if they could no longer keep them.

The Earl sat at the end of the table as the footmen hurried to bring back the dishes already sent to the kitchen.

Without being told the butler poured him a glass of champagne.

"Two-and-a-half hours," he boasted. "I believe no one before has ever done it in under three."

"That was very clever of you, Georgie. But as you have such superlative horses, you are not likely to have any challengers."

"That is very true, Galina, and when we go back to London and you are with me you will realise how excellent they really are."

"Don't let's talk of returning to London yet, I was just thinking as I was walking round the garden how lovely and peaceful it is here and how much happier I am at home in the country than anywhere else."

"You will have to complete the Season in the same style as you began it. Everyone is talking about you and three tiresome young gentlemen have already asked me if they can have your hand in marriage."

"I well know who they are and the answer is *'no'*!" Galina stipulated firmly. "Do please send them away and tell them to stop worrying me."

"They are just paying you a compliment, my dear beautiful sister. Most young women would be delighted to be in your shoes at the moment."

Galina looked at him enquiringly.

"You are the toast of White's," he continued, "and for that matter the whole of St. James's. Only last night His Royal Highness, the Prince of Wales, stopped me and congratulated me on my gorgeous sister."

"Did he really?"

"He did, and it made me certain you must be well chaperoned if he asks you to Marlborough House which he certainly intends to do!"

Galina laughed.

"I am quite safe, His Royal Highness has no use for *debutantes*. He has more beautiful women round him than most men can find in a hundred years!"

"That is certainly true. At the same time you will find yourself losing your reputation."

"You need not worry about me, Georgie, I was just thinking this morning that I prefer the lawn to a dance floor and our horses to the men I have met so far!"

"That is not the right attitude, Galina, but then you always see things differently to anyone else."

"I think we both do, but seriously I want to talk to you when you can spare the time."

"Why not now, Galina, I do not want any more to eat and I do like to take my time over a glass of port."

The port was poured into a glass and the decanter set down in front of him.

As the butler and the footmen withdrew, the pantry door closed behind them.

Then Georgie asked her,

"What is worrying you? Is it a man?"

Galina shook her head.

"No," she replied, "it is *money*."

Her brother raised his eyebrows.

"Do you need some? I thought I had paid all your bills."

"You have, but I'm quite certain, Georgie dear, that we are spending too much. We ought to try to make some economies."

"Strangely enough, Galina, you are taking the very words out of my mouth. When I was coming here today, I considered how much opening Ranmore House has cost us. And the bills for food and wine seem extraordinarily high."

"That is just what I was thinking."

"It would not have worried me so much, if I had not yesterday bought the Duke of Lockwood's stud, who if you remember died three weeks ago."

"You bought *all* the Lockwood racehorses?" Galina asked in astonishment.

"I have bought everything he possessed, lock, stock and barrel. I achieved a special price because they did not have to be auctioned at Tattersall's. It's an amazing deal – but equally somewhat expensive."

Galina drew in her breath.

"It must have cost you a fortune, but it is the most exciting news I have heard for a long time!"

"You will be thrilled with them. I went down to the country to see them and I knew that I would be a fool if I missed this opportunity of a lifetime."

"Of course, you would, Georgie, and the new Duke must have been very pleased with the transaction."

"He was absolutely delighted, for the simple reason he never cared for racing and thought it would be a bore to sell his horses off one by one!"

"So we have the whole lot," Galina said in an awed tone. "How many?"

"Over fifty and that includes not just the racehorses, but the hunters and, of course, all his carriage horses which are nearly as good as mine."

For a moment there was a silence and then Galina asked in a small voice,

"How are you going to pay for them?"

"That naturally is the most important question, but driving down I had an idea, which, if you can help me, I think will pay for this large new expense."

He took a deep breath before he continued,

"It could also make it possible to carry out the plans you and I have contemplated for some time – building our own Racecourse and increasing the size of the estate."

Galina gave a little gasp.

"That is indeed part of my dreams, but something I thought would never come true."

"As you well know, the land we want to buy will soon be put up for sale."

Galina shook her head as she cried,

"Oh, Georgie, if we could add not only the land we

want but the huge lake and the river with plenty of fish! It would make the whole place perfect."

"I agree with you and that is why I need your help."

"I am always ready to help, Georgie, but I cannot see how."

"I will tell you how and I want you to listen to me very carefully."

Galina put her elbows on the table to rest her chin on her hands.

"I am listening to every word," she breathed.

He paused for a moment and then began,

"I expect you know as everyone else does that it is becoming very fashionable for aristocrats who are feeling the pinch to look to America for a wife who is an heiress."

"Yes, of course. I have heard people talking about it, but I cannot believe you are thinking of such a course."

There was a note of horror in her voice which her brother did not miss.

"No, of course not. I am not thinking of marrying anyone let alone an American, who would not understand or even like everything that matters so much to us."

Galina gave a sigh of relief.

"Go on, tell me more."

"Well. Two of my friends have gone to New York simply because they just cannot afford to live as they wish to without a great deal more money. No doubt as they both have titles, they will come back with an American wife and thousands of dollars to bless themselves with."

Galina's eyes were on her brother's and there was a worried look in them.

"I was dining, the other night," he continued, "and one of the guests was a fellow called Craig Farlow. He is an American and I thought an unusually interesting one. I learnt from my host that he is enormously rich – in fact a millionaire several times over."

Galina gave a little sigh.

"How can the Americans have so much money?"

"The answer to that question is quite simple," her brother replied. "The answer is *oil*!"

Galina thought for a moment and then remarked,

"I remember some years ago when oil was found in Pennsylvania and next in other places in Europe and it was prophesied that it would be of enormous use to industry."

"That is correct and no one knows how much oil is hidden under the earth."

He took a sip of his port before adding,

"Strange to relate they were all talking about it last night and they said that no physical or chemical property of oil has yet been found which enables it to be detected from the surface."

"I suppose you mean that they just have to dig and hope for the best."

"That is right and very hard work it apparently is. Equally Farlow was telling us that he had been extremely lucky in finding well after well which, of course, accounts for him being so rich."

"Then why has he come to England!"

The Earl smiled.

"Need you ask? He has a daughter of twenty and as he is so fond of her, you can guess what he is looking for."

Galina looked at her brother.

"I suppose a title. Georgie, you are not thinking – "

"No, of course not. I have no intention of marrying anyone, as I said before, and certainly not an American."

"Then how does Mr. Farlow affect us?"

"He was saying at the party how much he disliked staying in hotels and how he found London hotels nothing like as good as New York's. After dinner I talked to him."

"And what did you say?"

There was a frightened look in her eyes. It was as if she believed her brother was going to spring something on her of which she would thoroughly disapprove.

"I suggested to Mr. Farlow," he replied, "that as we had just reopened Ranmore House in Park Lane, which is much too big for ourselves and our relatives, that he would find it very much more comfortable than a London hotel.

"I told him that the house was filled with servants and the reception rooms were at his disposal. Also there are plenty of bedrooms for any of his friends."

"Georgie, I just cannot believe it! What use is this to us?"

"That is what I am going to tell you, and you must let me do it in my own way step by step."

"Did Mr. Farlow accept?"

"He accepted with great alacrity. He wants to show off his daughter and somehow ingratiate himself into the Social world. He can do this very much more successfully from our house than from a hotel."

There was silence for a moment and then he added,

"I think you will find all the expenses of Ranmore House will now be paid for by Mr. Farlow."

"It is certainly a good idea in one way," said Galina after a lengthy pause. "But I think we may find it rather inconvenient to have him there all the time."

"You have not heard the end of my story, Galina, as whilst Mr. Farlow is exploring London and discovering an aristocratic son-in-law, I am going to America."

If he had laid a bomb at her feet, Galina could not have been more surprised.

"*America*!" she exclaimed. "Why on earth should you want to go there?"

"To find oil," her brother answered her calmly.

"How can you possibly find oil when there must be millions of Americans looking for oil in the same way as Mr. Farlow?"

"He found it, so why not me?"

"I think you are mad, Georgie, you know nothing about oil. How can you possibly walk into America, say that you are looking for oil and find a well?"

"I am not as stupid as that. Now just listen, Galina, this is where you come in."

She gazed at him.

Now she was feeling upset and in fact she thought to herself that her brother must have gone crazy.

"Last night," he began, "Mr. Craig Farlow, having enjoyed quite a lot of our host's good wine, became very talkative. He was asked how he managed to become so rich. He explained boastingly, but in an amusing manner that made everyone laugh, how he had outwitted other men like himself who were anxious to be millionaires."

"And *how* did he do it?" Galina asked in rather a hostile manner.

"He employed spies who located oil fields for him in Ohio, Illinois, Pennsylvania and Kansas."

"*Spies*! What do you mean?"

"They were, of course, men who studied the ground and who had some idea where there might be oil.

"They are the so-called 'wild-catters' because they drill for oil more in hope than with knowledge and without any geographical indications."

14

"But they succeed?"

"According to Farlow in a most amazing way. One after another the wild-catters seem almost by some instinct to find oil where no one expected it!"

"And you really think this is something you too can do?" Galina asked scornfully. "Mr. Farlow may have been fortunate, but that is just unusual and outstanding luck. For every Farlow who strikes oil, there must be thousands of drillers who fail to find anything."

"That is indeed true and Farlow said very much the same thing. But he believes in his luck and so do I."

"And how does that affect you?"

She was feeling somewhat aggressive, thinking that her brother had been deceived or just swept away by Mr. Farlow.

It was quite ridiculous to think that he might be as lucky. How could he be?

He would be a stranger in a strange land knowing nothing about what he was seeking.

"From what I learnt," Georgie was saying, "because like most Americans, Farlow talked and went on talking. After his first success he organised a whole gang of wild-catters and paid them a fat fee to find the oil he wanted.

"He went on to tell us that even though he is now extremely successful, his wild-catters are still working for him. In fact as far as I can ascertain it is becoming almost a game."

"A game! What do you mean?"

"Farlow explained that when a wild-catter finds a place he thinks might contain oil, he sends him a telegram telling him of his discovery. Of course, it is in a disguised fashion so that only he knows what the telegram means."

"Then what happens?"

"He telegraphs back instructing him to go ahead. It seems a somewhat complicated system, but he said that it prevented him from having an unnecessary drilling, which costs money and made it very clear to the wild-catters that he was the boss."

"It sounds very American to me and it is something which would be quite impossible for you to follow."

"I agree with you," her brother replied surprisingly. "But this, my dear sister, is where *you* come in!"

She stared at him.

"In what way? You are surely not expecting me to go drilling."

"What I want you to do, my Galina, is quite simple. When a telegram arrives for Mr. Farlow, you telegraph me before he sees it, using a secret code to tell me where the oil has been discovered."

She regarded him as if she could not believe what she was hearing.

"How can I *possibly* do that?"

"Quite easily. I will find out before I leave what particular places in America Farlow is interested in at the moment. I will go there. All you have to tell me when his telegram comes, is whether I am in the right place or not and if it is where the wild-catters want to drill."

"But it cannot be as easy as that and just how can I possibly spy on him, when he is a guest in our house?"

"It is not exactly spying, Galina, it is just reading a telegram before he can see it. Alternatively, because he is only too willing to talk of his discoveries, he is very likely to tell you what he is doing. Therefore you will not have a guilty conscience for passing the information on to me."

"And when you do know where the oil is or thought to be – what are you going to do about it?"

"I shall either buy the piece of land before Farlow can do so or drill so near to where his wild-catter is drilling that there is every possibility of us both striking oil!"

He spoke firmly with a self-assurance his sister had never seen before.

At the same time she felt that there was something wrong with this idea and she did not want to take part in it.

As if her brother could read her thoughts, he added,

"It is quite simple, Galina. If you want the truth we have overspent our income in the last two years and now I have bought the Duke's horses, we have to find the money from somewhere or sell everything we possess."

He spoke quietly yet seriously and Galina asked,

"Is it really as bad as that?"

"I was thinking yesterday before I met Farlow that we might have to give up our racing stable and also forget any ideas of having our private Racecourse."

Galina gave a little cry.

"Oh, no, Georgie, we cannot possibly do that! We have planned it for so long and how could we part with the racehorses which Papa made one of the finest stables in the whole of England?"

"I agree with you totally, but horses do cost money. You know just as well as I do that we can sell very little of what is in the house that is not entailed."

This was indeed true and Galina sighed.

"The only possessions of any great value," he went on, "that are ours completely are our horses. So if it is a question of being really clever and drilling a well in which Farlow is interested before he drills himself, you need not be sorry for him. He has more money than he can spend in a thousand years!"

"I can well believe it, Georgie, but I still think it is a somewhat sneaky way of behaving."

"It is this or closing down at Newmarket!"

"We cannot do that!" exclaimed Galina. "Our Papa would turn in his grave."

"I know and that is why I have to save them for my son, if I ever have one."

Galina did not speak and he carried on,

"It is quite obvious I cannot afford to get married at the moment nor do I intend to do so. If I did have a wife, I would ask her to help me, but I do not think she would be as clever about it as you would be."

Galina made a helpless gesture with her hands.

She knew when her brother talked to her like this that she could not refuse him anything.

"Very well," she conceded. "I agree, but when will you be going to America?"

"Tomorrow or the next day."

"You must be joking, Georgie."

"What have I to wait for? I have told Farlow he can move into Ranmore House immediately. In fact I think he intends to do so today. I want you to return to London and make yourself pleasant. Also as the hostess you can make certain the letters and telegrams that arrive go to the right guests staying in the house!"

Galina rose from the table.

"I think you are asking too much of me, Georgie, "and I am afraid, desperately afraid, that something will go wrong."

"It's an even chance one way or the other. If it all goes wrong you know what we have to do, but if all it goes right, we shall be happy and comfortable for a long time."

As she had nothing further to say, Galina made a helpless gesture and walked out of the dining room.

She walked down the passage into the study where they usually sat when they were alone.

Georgie was just behind her and when they entered the room, he closed the door.

"I don't want you to be upset, dearest sister, but we have to face facts that we have overspent and whilst you have been a huge success in London, it costs money."

"I know, I know, Georgie, and I now suppose that I should not to have gone to London."

"That would have been incredibly stupid and would certainly have upset Mama and Papa if they had been alive. I just want you to help me to find a few oil wells. Heaven knows there are thousands of them being discovered in all parts of the world!"

He paused to look at Galina.

"I could of course go to Romania, Burma, Sumatra or Persia, but I know that will take time and I know no one in those countries. If I go to Pennsylvania to start with, I am certain I shall find quite a number of friends or enemies of Farlow, who will be only too pleased to meet me."

He walked towards the window before he added,

"Quite frankly I believe they *will* help me. No man becomes as rich as Farlow without having those who envy him and who actually hate him for being so successful. If I am tactful I shall enlist their help."

Galina knew this to be true.

She always found that her brother had a beguiling way of making people do what he wanted.

He would never shout at anyone and was seldom disagreeable – actually he charmed them.

She had seen both men and women who would do

nothing for anyone else become weak in his hands when he asked for their assistance.

She gave a deep sigh.

"Well, if you must, do go, Georgie, and I admit we must do everything in our power to save the horses, then I *will* help you."

"I thought that you would. You have always been a sport and that is more than I can say of most women."

"Now let's go over it very carefully, because I must not make a mistake. Have you any idea exactly what Mr. Farlow has in the telegrams he receives from those he calls the wild-catters?"

"He explained it all to me last night. He uses a very simple code that does not in any way refer to oil. It varies, I gather, from a telegram reading,

'Have found the shawl you wanted for mother in a small village in Pennsylvania.'

To something like,

"Have found comfortable lodgings in the outskirts of Ohio."

"Oh, I see. The wild-catters are moving about."

"There are a good number of them, I do gather, and when they receive Farlow's permission they drill in a place wherever they are. So he telegraphs them saying,

'Thank you, do buy the shawl'."

"But how will you find out exactly where they are," Galina asked, "when there must be a great number of wild-catters in every place where they have already found oil?"

"That is a good question, but as we have already said, Americans talk. Those who work for Farlow, having been very successful already will undoubtedly be known to their unsuccessful neighbours. I would be very surprised if they did not boast of their own cleverness."

Galina thought that he had a point and after a little silence, she could only say,

"If I am not to fail you or make a mistake, please find out everything you can before you leave."

Then, as she suddenly thought of it, she added,

"Don't be away too long."

"I shall be content at the moment with just one oil well, but, of course, it depends how much it brings me. It does not take as long as it used to, now there are the new Steamers sailing backwards and forwards to America."

Galina knew he was right, but she felt nervous of being in London without her brother when the house would be filled with Mr. Farlow and his guests.

In a rather small voice she insisted,

"If you must go, Georgie, please, please come back as quickly as possible. I shall be so worried until you do."

"I promise you," her brother answered, "I will not wait one moment after I realise I am a millionaire!"

CHAPTER TWO

Thanks to Galina's pleading they stayed the next day at home.

They rode the horses and looked at the acres of land that joined them that they wished to buy.

As she rode back home Galina felt assured that she was doing the right thing in helping her brother find an oil well.

"You must give me time to meet Mr. Farlow," she suggested. "Because the idea scares me, as you know."

"You will manage it, Galina, if you can conquer the Social world of London, you can certainly conquer just one American!"

"I can only hope your prediction comes true, but it is not going to be easy."

They drove off again for London with a new team, but they did not beat the record this time as there seemed to be more traffic.

When her brother drew up with a flourish outside Ranmore House in Park Lane, Galina clapped her hands.

"That was a wonderful drive," she enthused, "and I congratulate you. If we finally lose all our money, you can always get a job as a coachman!"

Leaving the horses with a groom, they walked into the house.

The butler bowed to them and the Earl asked him,

"Is Mr. Farlow here?"

"He's in the study, my Lord."

The Earl gave his sister a quick glance.

She guessed he was thinking that Mr. Farlow might be either reading important letters or perhaps making out the telegrams he wanted to send.

The butler opened the study door and they entered.

Galina was not quite certain what she expected Mr. Farlow to look like.

But there was no doubt from the first glance that he was American and a businessman from the top of his head to the soles of his feet.

As he rose from an armchair to meet them, she saw he was not very tall and rather sparingly built.

He was the type of man who would walk quickly as his brain was working quickly.

"I was just wondering when you'd get back," Mr. Farlow addressed the Earl.

"I promised you that I would not be long and I have brought my sister, who is going to look after you with me. So you will be even more comfortable than you are at the moment."

"That would be quite impossible," Mr. Farlow said genially.

He shook hands with Galina saying,

"It's a real pleasure to meet you, Lady Ranmore."

Galina looked at her brother, who remarked,

"I must explain to you, Craig, that my sister is Lady Galina More. She is not allowed to use the whole of our name."

The American laughed.

"You'll have to teach me all the pros and cons now I'm in England. As we don't have any titles in America, I'm very ignorant of them I can assure you."

"Well, as you are so good in the business world, we just cannot expect you to know all the ridiculous rules that exist in the Social one. But I assure you my sister will put you and your daughter right, so that you will not make any mistakes."

"Is that a promise?" enquired Mr. Farlow.

"Of course it is," Galina assured him. "And do not worry about the English titles. They are very complicated and everyone coming from foreign parts makes mistakes at first. The only thing I can say is that we are not as bad as the Russians!"

Mr. Farlow threw up his hands.

"There I can agree with you, but I hears there's oil in the Caucasus, so perhaps I'll be going over there sooner or later."

Galina smiled at him.

"My brother, Georgie, has been telling me just how successful you are in America. It is very interesting to us as we have no oil in England so far, and I understand you only found yours a few years ago."

"That's very true and now there's too many people drilling for oil and I am only glad that I got in more or less at the beginning."

"I think that was very astute of you," Galina said flatteringly.

Mr. Farlow was still telling her how clever he had been when the door opened and his daughter came in.

He jumped up.

"Oh, here you are," he called out, "and now you are going to meet our hostess who is the Earl's sister."

He took his daughter by her right hand and drew her towards Galina who had also risen.

Ellie-May Farlow was not particularly exciting at first glance and she was dressed in a rather ugly manner.

Her hair was dark like her father's and it was not arranged in what in London was considered the most up-to-date style.

She had blue eyes and a not especially clear skin.

Whenever she smiled, however, she took on quite a fascinating expression that more or less altered her face.

Galina shook her by the hand saying,

"I am delighted you are staying here and I hope you will enjoy London."

"Papa is very anxious for me to do so," she replied.

Her accent was not so pronounced as her father's.

As she smiled, Galina felt she could be very much more attractive than she appeared.

While they were talking, the butler announced that tea was ready in the drawing room and they went upstairs.

Mr. Farlow explained that while he and Ellie-May were staying in the house the men he had brought with him were not. They were busy during the day carrying out his instructions, but they would be in for dinner.

Because Mr. Farlow wished to attend to some of his business, he went back to the study when tea was finished.

Galina chose her words carefully, but equally she thought that what she had to say would be what Mr. Farlow would expect from her.

"I think," she now said to Ellie-May, "that you and I must go shopping tomorrow."

Galina expected she might have to explain why, but Ellie-May replied,

"Papa told me you would help me when you arrived here. I know I need some different clothes. I bought these in America and I know I don't look right."

"If you are going to attend balls and parties here, you will find that most of the model dresses we wear come from Paris. I will take you to the very best shops in Bond Street that bring in all their prettiest gowns from France."

"That'll be fun, Lady Galina, and I'd like to look as smart as you if it's at all possible."

"It's just a question of your father paying the bills!"

"Oh, he'll do that all right! He's got pots of money as I expect he's told you and I want all the prettiest dresses you can buy me, so that I don't feel like a stranger if we go to any parties."

"Of course you are going to parties, Ellie-May, and I'm going to send tomorrow for London's best hairdresser. He is expensive, but he will make you look very smart."

Ellie-May clapped her hands together.

"This is real nice of you and it's the sort of thing I hoped would happen to me when I came to London."

"Now what is important," insisted Galina, "is that you make a good impression from the moment you appear anywhere, so we will do our shopping first thing tomorrow and only when you are fashionable and look your very best must you appear at any function."

"That's just what I would love and as I said it's real kind of you to take the trouble over me."

Ellie-May gave a little sigh.

"Having no mother makes things very difficult. If I travel with Papa, we move so quickly from place to place that I never have time to visit a shop."

"Well, we will make the time now you are here and I tell you what we will do. I'll suggest to my brother that he arranges a dinner party for tomorrow evening before we take you to whichever ball we are attending. There is sure to be one. But you must be transformed by that time!"

She knew as she spoke it would be a rush.

But if Georgie was talking of going to America, she had to make him start the ball rolling before he left.

When she accompanied Ellie-May upstairs to dress for dinner, she went to her brother's room.

He was, of course, sleeping where all his ancestors had slept in the Master Suite.

It was a very imposing room with a four-poster bed surrounded by red velvet curtains and with the family Coat of Arms embroidered over the headboard.

Georgie had, in fact, just finished his bath and was talking to his valet and when Galina appeared in the room, the valet discreetly went outside.

"I have done what you told me to do, Georgie," she began, "and I am taking Ellie-May to the shops tomorrow. But I thought that if you are going away, we had better have a dinner party tomorrow to include everyone who might be useful to them. You know far more people than I do."

"I had not thought of that, but you are right."

"I think too, though I have not had time to ask your secretary, that we have been asked to a ball tomorrow."

"You are so right again, Galina, and I will ask the Duchess if I can bring the Farlows."

"You don't think she will mind us pushing in?"

"Not when she realises how rich Farlow is, already people are talking about him. You will have no difficulty in introducing him to almost everyone in the *Beau Monde* and naturally when you give parties, they will all come with alacrity and doubtless with their hands open."

"They can hardly think they are going to get money from him!" exclaimed Galina.

Her brother laughed.

"There are plenty of ways and means. There are always people who have something to sell, whether it is a horse, a picture or a piece of jewellery which belonged to their great-grandmother!"

Galina giggled.

"I am sure you are right, Georgie."

"I expect Farlow is quite used to it and I bet that he never goes through an evening without someone trying to extort a few thousands from him."

"That makes me feel uncomfortable, but equally I hope we do not have to pay for the parties he gives here."

"Don't be silly. You don't suppose they are staying here for nothing."

"I thought they were – your guests."

"They are extremely grateful to me for letting them rent one of the most outstanding houses in Mayfair. But of course they are paying for the privilege and for the servants who wait on them."

Galina gave a little cry.

"Oh, Georgie, that *is* clever of you and I must say it takes some of the weight off my shoulders."

"I am going to see it is all removed," he answered. "But don't forget all you have to do and I think I shall have to leave for America on Friday at the latest."

"I think that is far too soon."

"Only from your point of view, my dear Galina. It is absolutely essential I should be there when you send me a telegram."

"But surely, Georgie, you are not going to tell Mr. Farlow where you are going!"

"I'm not a fool. As far as he is concerned I have got to run across to Paris at the request of the Secretary of State for Foreign Affairs. I shall be very apologetic, but it is an obligation I cannot refuse."

"You are too sharp for words, but be careful you don't cut yourself!"

Galina walked towards the door.

"I suppose it does not matter how much I spend on making Ellie-May look her best?"

"It is not going to be easy, as far as I am concerned, she is a rather plain American miss."

"That is the challenge and I will try to make you eat your words tomorrow night, Georgie!"

She left the room before her brother could answer, but she heard him laugh as she walked down the corridor to her own room.

Dinner that evening was rather dull, she thought.

The two young Americans who were working for Mr. Farlow came to dinner and they were not the least shy and talked volubly all through the meal.

It was all about their impressions of England and they thought that the businessmen in London were rather slow compared to those in America.

"We are an old country," Galina said to them, "so you really cannot expect us to rush about like you do. But nevertheless you will have to admit for a small island we have done pretty well!"

She was thinking as she spoke that over a quarter of the world now belonged to the British Empire and flew the Union Jack.

But it was a pity we had lost America.

Equally she had to admire the progress that country had made on its own.

She asked the young man sitting on her right what they were working on for Mr. Farlow.

She wondered if he would think she was prying, but he answered without hesitation,

"I and my friend have been engaged in finding the oil which has been so successful for Mr. Farlow. But he's never satisfied and now we are looking at other industries to see if they can produce the same return as oil has done."

"We have a number of new inventions in England like electric light and photography," suggested Galina.

"That's true," he responded, "but I don't see huge fortunes coming from them at the moment. I thinks myself that Mr. Farlow would do better with ships and some of the other larger industries that we are already investigating."

"I feel you are thinking that you are more advanced than we are in the development of Steamships."

He laughed at Galina's remark and then he turned to speak to the person on his other side.

Galina was quite certain then that Mr. Farlow was seriously interested in Steamships and he would doubtless make another fortune from having larger, faster and better ones than were being built in England.

As she went to bed, Galina felt that the Americans were actually going ahead almost too quickly – and it was frightening how much they had achieved already.

The fact they had oil while Britain had none might be a pointer that there must be hundreds of other activities in which, if they were ambitious, they might excel.

But for the moment it was no use worrying about it.

She had to concentrate on helping Georgie.

*

The next morning Galina and Ellie-May set off in a stylish open carriage drawn by two horses to Bond Street.

It was not far, but Galina thought they should look right.

She took Ellie-May to the smartest and actually the most expensive shop in Bond Street. In this shop she had bought the gown she had been presented in and two other evening gowns.

She was too poor to buy any more even though she knew the clothes were lovely and suited her.

Galina explained to the vendeuse that Miss Farlow required what might almost be described as a trousseau.

The whole shop seemed to fly into action – gowns were brought to them from every direction as mannequins paraded in front of them.

Ellie-May wished to look totally different and the clothes transformed her as if she was touched by a magic wand.

They had bought twenty gowns and day dresses by luncheon time.

The most important, which naturally was the most expensive, was to be ready for Ellie-May this evening.

They returned to Ranmore House for luncheon and Galina was feeling exhausted by the morning's activity, but Ellie-May was ready to go on in the afternoon.

"I am taking you to a hat shop this afternoon," said Galina, "then I am coming home to rest. We have a party tonight and I find that buying clothes is far more tiring than riding for hours as I do at home."

"I think it's real kind of you to take all this trouble, Lady Galina, but I do need some hats and shoes to go with all the beautiful dresses."

After luncheon they went to the best hat shop where the proprietress had already found out that money was no object.

They were bowed into the shop almost as if they were Royalty and Ellie-May was the focus of attention for the two hours they were there.

Afterwards they bought shoes and long kid gloves, which were not the fashion in America.

It was teatime before they were back in Park Lane.

Galina flopped onto a sofa and asked Ellie-May to pour out the tea.

"I am exhausted, but I can see you are as fresh as a daisy!"

"It's all so exciting," enthused Ellie-May. "I never knew that clothes could be so fabulous or so very different to everything I had bought myself in New York."

"From what you have told me I would think New York must be behind Europe in women's clothes if nothing else, but doubtless when you go back you can start a new fashion and your father will make millions of dollars out of the fashion business!"

"He would like that. Papa chases money and the more he gets the happier he is."

"He is a very shrewd man."

"He sure is!"

Galina wondered if she should tell Ellie-May that what she had just said was not a very pretty remark.

There were a number of American expressions that sounded rather grating when they were spoken in London.

Then she told herself it was too soon. She must not embarrass Ellie-May in any manner or make her over self-conscious about herself.

Galina had found out that the American girl was far more intelligent than she expected her to be and she had an enthusiasm for everything that was rather touching.

With tea over Galina insisted they went upstairs to rest until the hairdresser came.

"I expect he will take an hour over you," she said to Ellie-May, "and will be far quicker with me, so you shall have him first. Then you must put on the best gown which we have chosen for you to wear tonight."

"Supposing it doesn't fit?"

"It will," Galina reassured her. "It is too expensive for the shop to make any mistakes, so you need not worry."

Just as Ellie-May was leaving her, she asked,

"Have you any jewellery?"

Ellie-May nodded.

"Lots of it, but Papa thought it would be a mistake, as I am unmarried, for me to wear too much."

"He is quite right, but bring out what you have and we will choose a necklace and perhaps a bracelet for you to wear with the new gown."

"I have all the jewels which Papa gave my mother, but I don't want to look vulgar, so you must choose what is suitable for me."

"I will do so," promised Galina. "Now go and rest in your room until the hairdresser arrives. Remember he has a high opinion of himself, as he is in demand from the Princess of Wales and all the top actresses in London."

"I'll kow-tow to him all right. We've got plenty of people like that in New York and they are not happy unless you're going down on your knees in front of them!"

She disappeared before Galina could answer.

She thought with satisfaction that Ellie-May had an excellent sense of humour that would help her more than anything else.

There was little doubt that Monsieur Hemes was a genius as when Galina went to Ellie-May's bedroom after he had been with her for half-an-hour, he had performed one of his miracles.

Ellie-May's dark hair was beautifully arranged in the very latest fashion and yet it appeared to be unique and it completely altered her appearance.

It made her face seem thinner and her body smaller, but at the same time she had an elegance which could only have come from Paris.

While Monsieur Hemes stood back to wait for the compliments, Galina paid him.

"I think, monsieur, we must ask you to call in every day. No one but you could possibly make the hair dance on Miss Farlow as you have done and she will undoubtedly be the 'belle of the ball' this evening."

"That will be difficult if you are there, my Lady," he replied. "But she will be a good runner-up!"

Galina laughed.

She knew that in using the slang of the Racecourse, Monsieur Hemes's main interest, apart from hairdressing, was racing.

Ellie-May was delighted with herself and thanked Monsieur Hemes profusely.

When Galina ran back to her own room he followed and arranged her hair.

"Am I right, my Lady," he asked, "in believing that the father of the lady whose lovely hair I have just arranged is the American millionaire everyone is talking about."

"Mr. Farlow has not been in London long, so I am surprised people are already talking about him, but he is, in fact, a millionaire from Pennsylvania."

"Money always talks, my Lady, and I have heard of him from quite a number of my customers."

Galina thought that as he would certainly add to the gossip, she only said,

"I am sure, monsieur, that Mr. Farlow will be very

grateful to you for what you have done for his daughter. My brother has suggested that, as you will be calling here every day, you should hand the secretary your bill at the end of each week."

She realised by the expression on Monsieur Hemes face that this satisfied him, because it meant there would be no arguments about his charges.

Also if Ellie-May did not see the bill, she would not be able to complain that it was too much.

Monsieur Hemes had finished Galina's hair and she looked even lovelier than she was already.

She dressed in the glamorous gown she had chosen before she went to Ellie-May's room.

Ellie-May had finished having her hands manicured by her lady's maid and was ready but for her jewellery.

What she possessed was spread out on the table and when she saw it, Galina drew in her breath.

Never had she imagined that a girl of Ellie-May's age would possess so much or such valuable jewels and the expression on her face must have told Ellie-May what she was thinking.

"Papa gave my mother a piece of jewellery every time he pulled off a good deal or found a new oil well."

They were certainly spectacular presents.

There were necklaces of huge diamonds and other precious stones as well as bracelets, ear-rings and rings that looked almost too heavy for a slim female finger.

Galina dismissed them as too grand until she found a pretty necklace of one row of pearls.

Ellie-May laughed.

"I thought you'd choose those. I just put out the emeralds and diamonds for you to see them."

"I think they are magnificent," sighed Galina. "But you must be careful they are not stolen."

"The Earl told me to put them in the safe."

"And that is exactly where they must stay, although I would have thought the bank would be even safer."

She realised as she spoke that Ellie-May was not interested – she was looking for a rather simple bracelet of just one row of diamonds.

And then she looked up at Galina enquiringly,

"This is one of the presents Papa gave Mama before he found oil. Is it too much for me?"

As it was a simple bracelet Galina advised,

"No, do wear it and if you have another like it, you could put it on your other wrist."

It was however still more than an English *debutante* should wear, but equally, as Ellie-May was American and the daughter of a very rich father, people would expect her to be somewhat bejewelled.

Ellie-May did exactly as she was told and then she looked rather wistfully at the other jewels as they were shut up one by one in their boxes.

"Now we must go downstairs," suggested Galina. "Our guests will be arriving at any time and I am sure my brother is there waiting for us."

They walked down to the reception room.

When Georgie saw the new Ellie-May, he stared at her in sheer astonishment and then he said to Galina,

"You did not tell me we had a new beauty staying with us! Please introduce me!"

Ellie-May giggled coquettishly.

"That's the sort of compliment I want to have!"

"Well, I am certain you will get plenty this evening.

All I can say is that my sister is a witch and in medieval times she would surely have been burnt at the stake. She has just transformed you from an ordinary American girl into an irresistible beauty."

Ellie-May threw up her hands.

"Do tell me more! More and more! That's the real McCoy and just what I want to hear."

They were all laughing as the butler announced the first guest.

Because Georgie had been out all day, Galina had not had a chance to ask him who he had invited.

She realised as the guests arrived one after another that they were all titled and as far as she could remember, in need of money.

They were about the same age as her brother and she thought most of them must have been at Eton with him.

As they arrived in couples, she realised he had told them to bring with them some girl they liked who would be about the same age as Ellie-May.

Doubtless later they would ask her to any party they were giving and it was an intelligent idea and typical, she thought, of her brother.

She was thinking it was time they went into dinner when the last guest arrived.

He was a tall, handsome gentleman and unlike the rest of the party, he had come alone.

"Lord Bramton, my Lady," the butler announced.

Galina, who was at the other end of the room turned round and walked towards him.

As she drew nearer she noticed he was extremely handsome and she then wondered why she had not met him before.

Georgie reached the newcomer before she did.

"I am very glad you could come, Victor. I asked at your Club, but they were not certain if you were returning today or tomorrow."

"I was delighted to hear from you," he replied.

"I do not think you have met my sister. Galina, this is Victor Bramton whose house in Lincolnshire rivals ours in age and it always annoyed Papa that it was older!"

"But not in such a good condition," Lord Bramton commented as he took Galina's hand.

Then she looked up into his eyes.

For a moment she felt as if the world stood still.

It was a strange feeling she had never felt before.

She was acutely aware of his fingers on her hand.

His whole being seemed to vibrate towards her.

Then the butler's stentorian voice proclaimed,

"Dinner is served, my Lady."

They all went into dinner and Galina found she was sitting with two Peers on either side of her.

At the head of the table Georgie had Ellie-May on his right and a lovely *debutante*, who was to have several balls given for her, on his left.

There was no one elderly and Craig Farlow did not appear.

The dinner was superb and the gentlemen, as they all knew each other well, were talking away nineteen to the dozen. In fact, they were more interested in what they had to say to each other than in the girls sitting beside them.

Galina was delighted to note that Ellie-May stood out even amongst the prettiest of this Season's *debutantes* and she also realised as the evening went on that she was not shy – with encouragement she had a great deal to say for herself.

'She will be a success,' Galina thought, 'even apart from all the money that lies behind her.'

With his unusual efficiency Georgie had arranged for the correct number of carriages to be waiting for them outside after dinner as they were all going to a ball given by the Duke and Duchess of Bedford.

Galina saw that all her guests were settled first and then she climbed into the last carriage.

Inside was Lord Bramton and Galina realised as the guests paired themselves off that Lord Bramton made the extra partner for her.

Her brother had his special lady friend, a girl he had danced with quite a lot before they had gone to the country.

She was certainly very pretty but, Galina thought a little sadly, there was no chance of Georgie marrying her, even if he wanted to.

Her parents were too poor to throw a ball for her during the Season and it was just because she was so lovely that she was asked to most balls even though she could not return the invitations.

As the horses started off, Galina was acutely aware of Lord Bramton sitting beside her.

She could not explain to herself why she had this feeling about him, yet it was undoubtedly there.

Turning to him she enquired,

"You must be an old friend of my brother's, but it is strange that we have never met before."

"I have seen you in the distance," he replied, "but as you had a large attendance of gentlemen around you, I did not interrupt."

Galina laughed.

"That does sound so glamorous, but actually there were too many of them, so I ran away to the country!"

"I wondered why I had not seen you again."

"I am flattered you should notice me."

He smiled at her.

"Now you are fishing for compliments. You know that you are undoubtedly the belle of the Season and your brother, whom I have known for many years, is very proud of you."

"I hope so, because I am proud of him too and I do think he has organised this evening very well."

"He told me he was doing it for the rich Mr. Farlow and that you have him and his daughter staying at Ranmore House."

"I find them very interesting," Galina told him.

"And I am sure that they are very grateful to you. I cannot imagine that any American lady would look as Miss Farlow does this evening without your help."

"It is very nice of you to think so, but I have made her look more English and less American."

"I did notice it, as soon as I saw her."

"That is a compliment to Ellie-May," Galina added, "but not particularly to America!"

Lord Bramton smiled.

"I have been to America and I know what the girls look like. But that, of course, is very different to the way Miss Farlow looks this evening."

"As I have already said it is clever of you to realise what has happened, but you must not mention it to anyone else because it might be embarrassing for Ellie-May."

"You know very well that I would not do anything to hurt you," murmured Lord Bramton.

The way he spoke made Galina feel a strange flutter in her heart.

It was different from anything she had felt before.

"If you are an old friend of my brother's, why have I not met you before," she asked him again coyly.

There was a pause before he replied,

"It is a rather sad story which I will tell you another time if you are willing to listen."

"Of course I am, and you are making me curious."

"You are exactly what I expected you to be. That is why if I had any commonsense, I would not have accepted Georgie's invitation here this evening."

Galina looked at him in surprise.

"Why?" she asked.

Even as she spoke, the carriage drew up outside the Duke of Bedford's house.

A footman hurried to open the door of the carriage and there was no chance of saying any more.

As she was about to step out, Galina knew that she wanted to go on talking to Lord Bramton.

In fact she was so anxious to do so that she became suddenly frightened that she might not see him again.

Without even thinking what she was saying, as they walked in through the front door, she whispered,

"Please do not disappear. There is so much I want to say to you."

For a moment their eyes met.

Then he said quietly,

"That is exactly what I wanted you to say."

CHAPTER THREE

The Duke of Bedford's house was impressive, but Galina thought not as well furnished as theirs.

It was a large party and the Duchess, looking very attractive in white, was receiving her guests, most of them young, as her daughter had been presented at the same time as Galina.

The moment Galina moved into the large ballroom, a number of men hurried towards her to ask for a dance.

She introduced them to Ellie-May, who was beside her and she was glad that they were obviously delighted to ask her to dance.

And Ellie-May's dance card was quickly filled up.

It was then that Galina found herself dancing with one the young gentleman who had already proposed to her.

"I have been thinking of you all day," he enthused, "and I cannot think how I could be so lucky as to have the first dance with you."

"As a matter of fact I do believe we started dancing without you even asking me!"

"I had to snatch my opportunity rather than leave it to fate," he replied.

"Do you usually do that?" enquired Galina.

He shook his head.

"Fate is not always kind to me and like you usually prefers to wait before she gives me a reply to my prayers."

Galina realised that he was going to propose to her again, so she quickly changed the subject,

"I want you to be nice to Miss Farlow, who I have brought with me tonight. You might know that she is the daughter of the American oil multi-millionaire everyone is talking about. I think you will find her very charming."

"I don't want Miss Farlow, I want *you*."

It was no use trying to talk to him about anyone but themselves and as soon as the dance had ended, Galina was glad when she was claimed by another young gentleman.

He said she had promised him the first dance when she came back to London.

"I cannot remember that and I am sure it is untrue," Galina answered him.

"It is true, Galina," he insisted, "and as I have been deprived of the first dance, I insist on having the second."

There was no chance for her first partner to protest that she should stay with him until the music started, as the second young man swept Galina away at the first note.

She noted that Ellie-May was not only dancing but also talking animatedly, so she need not worry about her.

Ellie-May certainly looked exceedingly attractive in her new dress with her hair so beautifully arranged by the famous Monsieur Hemes.

Galina was quite certain that Ellie-May would not be a wallflower.

Galina had danced four dances when, as it was very hot, she went into the garden for a breath of fresh air.

"Would you like something to drink?" her partner asked.

"I would love a glass of lemonade," replied Galina.

He looked round and saw there was an empty seat under a tree decorated with Chinese lanterns.

"Wait there, and I will be as quick as I can."

He went away.

Then, to Galina's surprise, Lord Bramton appeared apparently from nowhere.

"I have been waiting," he began, "to find you alone. Now come quickly because I do want to talk to you."

Galina realised she was behaving badly in running away from her partner, but she really could not resist Lord Bramton's invitation.

Almost before she could guess what was happening her hand was in his and he was leading her quickly through the trees.

He took her to a part of the garden that was not lit with fairy lights.

There was, however, a pale moon coming out in the starlit sky and it enabled Lord Bramton to find a seat in a group of rhododendrons that would hide them from other people wandering about.

As they sat down, Galina piped up,

"I suppose you do know you are making me behave badly. In fact, I am being very rude to my last partner."

"It was the only chance of getting you to myself," Lord Bramton muttered, "and you know that we have not yet finished our conversation."

"That's true, but we will have to think of some very good excuse as to why I vanished."

"If he has any sense he will believe you have gone back to Olympus from whence you came!"

Galina laughed.

"I am quite prepared to be a Goddess, but I would like to be one of the better behaved ones!"

"I am very certain that nothing you did could ever be wrong – "

Galina laughed again.

"That is just the sort of compliment I like, but I only wish it was true."

"I have been looking for you for a long time," Lord Bramton breathed, "and when I saw you tonight I could not believe you were true."

He spoke seriously and for some reason she could not understand she felt as if her heart gave a little quiver.

"I don't think – I understand what you mean."

"Why should you, dear Galina? But it happens to be true that you are even more beautiful than you were in my imagination and when I talked to you at dinner, I knew that I no longer had to go on dreaming of the impossible."

Because he spoke so fervently, Galina could not for the moment think what to say.

Again she could feel that strange sensation within herself.

"I will now tell you the answer to your question of why we have not met before. It is because I cannot afford to come to London and as I cannot offer my friends any hospitality, I do not accept theirs."

Galina looked at him in astonishment.

"Are you saying, in a rather strange way, that you are very poor?"

"That, if anything, is an exaggeration. I am almost penniless and I cannot think what I can do about it."

Galina drew in her breath.

"But Georgie has told me that you have one of the most famous and beautiful houses in England."

"That is true, but I have no way of keeping it up. I think I shall just have to close the doors and live in one of the cottages."

"But you cannot do such a thing! There must be some way that you can sell something even if it is a piece of the estate."

She was thinking of hers and Georgie's problems as she spoke.

Lord Bramton shook his head.

"No! As I expect you understand I personally own nothing, not even a picture or one inch of land."

Galina recognised at once it was the same problem facing her and Georgie.

Yet her brother believed he had a chance of making some money by going to America, but that was something she could not say to Lord Bramton.

"I am sorry, I am desperately sorry for you, but I do understand because everything Georgie owns is entailed."

"I know because I have often talked about it with him and wondered if there was any solution – "

"There must be something you can do."

"If there was, I am sure I would have thought of it."

There was silence for a moment and then he said,

"Now, to make me even more miserable than I am already, I have found *you*!"

Galina looked at him and then looked away.

Even in the moonlight she could see only too well from the expression in his eyes what he was feeling.

"You are so exquisitely beautiful," Lord Bramton was saying in a deep voice. "And when we met I thought there was a celestial light behind your head and you were not human but Divine."

"You must not say such words to me – "

"Why not?" he asked. "I have nothing else to offer you and perhaps after tonight we will never meet again."

Galina gave a little cry.

She did not know why, but she wanted to meet him again.

It seemed so extraordinary she should feel like this, but then it was so extraordinary that any man she had just met should speak to her as Lord Bramton was doing.

"It's not just because of your incredible beauty," he was saying, "but I feel when I touch your hand, as if I was joined to you spiritually and that nothing can divide us."

Galina drew in her breath.

She felt as if her heart reached out towards him.

She understood, although she did not really want to, exactly what he was saying.

Looking away from him, she mumbled,

"You must not think about me, but of some solution to your problem."

"I have thought and thought," he answered, "and I swear there is no solution."

There was silence for a moment, then he remarked,

"Of course, I suppose I could cheat and try to sell things that are entailed and hope no one will find me out."

He paused, sighed and then continued,

"But if they did, I would be disgraced and even if I got away with it, I should be ashamed of myself and the family whose name I bear."

"No, of course you cannot do anything crooked any more than we can. We have been brought up to be ladies and gentlemen and that is just what we have to be, however much we may suffer."

Lord Bramton smiled sadly.

"I knew that you would understand, as no one else would."

Galina suddenly gave a little cry.

"I have thought of a solution, but you may not like it. However, it would save you and your house, those who belong to you and your children when you have them."

Lord Bramton stared at her.

"You have a solution!" he repeated as if he could not believe what she had just said. "What is it?"

"You must marry Ellie-May. Her father wants her to marry someone with a title and although you are only a Lord, no one has a house to compare with yours."

"I have no wish to marry anyone except *you*," Lord Bramton exclaimed.

Galina looked horrified.

There was a poignant silence and then he blurted out passionately,

"How could I marry anyone when I love *you*?"

"How could you ever say that when you have only just met me?" she asked with a puzzled look on her face.

Lord Bramton looked up to the sky.

"I swear to you on everything I hold sacred that I have never been in love until this very minute. When I saw you tonight with that celestial light behind you, I knew it was a miracle and I had found what I have been seeking."

"How can you say that?" Galina asked him again.

"I can say it because it is true, Galina. Of course, I have had the opportunity of marrying young girls who have come to admire my house and whose parents have thought it would be very pleasant for them to own it with me."

"I think people have felt the same about Georgie."

As if she had not spoken, Lord Bramton continued,

"In the back of my mind I have always realised it would be quite wrong to marry without love – the real love

I have certainly *never* felt for any of the women who have tried to flirt with me."

"But how can you be sure that what you feel for me is not just a passing fad? Like something which comes to you after a good dinner."

"Give me your hand, Galina – "

Because it seemed somehow to be a command, she put out her left hand and he took it in both of his.

His fingers closed over it.

She then felt – although she thought that she must be imagining it – another even stranger vibration running through her entire body.

It was a sensation that seemed to become a thrill.

It touched her heart and then her lips.

Lord Bramton did not speak, but just looked at her.

Then unexpectedly he took his hands away.

"Now you understand!"

"I do not!" Galina protested. "How can you do that to me?"

Lord Bramton smiled.

"You are feeling just what I am feeling and perhaps because you are so young, you have not yet recognised it as *love* – the true love we all seek."

Galina did not say anything and he went on,

"We were made for each other and I do believe we have been together in another life."

He paused and then he murmured in a voice of deep emotion,

"Now I have found you again and there is nothing I can do about it."

It was impossible for Galina to speak.

She was so astonished at the way she had just felt.

"I love you," he breathed. "I know if it was at all possible for us to be together, we would be supremely and divinely happy."

"If you feel like that," said Galina in a very small voice, "there must be something you can do about it."

"There are only two things I can do. One is to take you in my arms and kiss you until you love me as much as I love you, or secondly to disappear so that you will never see me again."

"But I do want to see you again – "

It was something she had not meant to say.

Yet somehow the words came into her lips and she could not prevent herself.

"My darling, my sweet one. You are everything I knew you would be if I could find you. But now I know if I was to behave properly, I would go away and you would never have to think about me again."

"But where would you go and what would you do?"

"Does it really matter? As far as I am concerned, the sooner I am dead the better!"

"That is a wicked thing to say," she asserted, "and I am surprised you can be so faint-hearted."

He looked at her in astonishment.

"Faint-hearted!" he exclaimed.

"If you really love me as you say you do," Galina answered him, "I am sure there is something we can think of together that will save your house and you."

Lord Bramton reached out and took her hand back into his and kissed it.

At the touch of his lips on her skin, she felt a strong heat course through her.

She sensed, although it seemed unbelievable, that he was right and that they were really meant for each other.

"I just worship and adore you," Lord Bramton said, "and now because I feel you have more commonsense than I have, tell me what we must do."

It then flashed through Galina's mind that he could appeal to Mr. Farlow for help.

But that might in some way upset Georgie's plans.

She was not certain how, but it would be a mistake for too many plots to be going on at the same time.

"There must be some way that you could find help. I am sure if we pray very hard an idea will come to us. But while we are waiting for an answer to our prayers, we must not do anything foolish."

"Are you suggesting that I should stay in London and see you?" he asked.

"Why not?"

"I am staying at my Club, but I cannot really afford it anymore."

"Then what you must do is to move into Ranmore House!"

Lord Bramton stared at her.

"Do you really mean it?"

"I can see no reason why you should not. Georgie is going away for a short time. Anyway there is plenty of room and everything is paid for by Mr. Farlow."

As she spoke she felt certain that Mr. Farlow would undoubtedly be delighted to entertain any young gentleman with a title.

Something else passed through her mind.

Perhaps if he was there and seeing Ellie-May every day, Lord Bramton might think after all he should marry her and forget his dreams of perfect love.

Even as she was mulling over the idea, he shook his head.

"That will not happen, Galina."

"You cannot be reading my thoughts!"

"I can read your thoughts just as if you tried to, you would find you could read mine. We belong to each other, my beautiful Goddess, and whatever happens in the future we will still belong even if fate takes us from each other."

"If you really do believe that, and somehow you are making me feel it is true, then I feel sure that we shall find a solution to your problem and to Georgie's. At least we can try."

"Of course we can," Lord Bramton agreed, "but it is going to be hard, very hard not to tell you how much I love you and make you love me as I want you to do."

"I know just what you are saying, but do you think it would be somewhat unfair to make me love you when you cannot afford to marry me."

"Now you are reading *my* thoughts, Galina, and if I do come to stay at Ranmore House, it will be hell for me to behave as you want me to, although at the same time it will be Heaven to be near you."

"Then let's try it," Galina pleaded, "and perhaps as you believe we have been so lucky to find each other, then why should not God, who is guiding us, be kinder still?"

"We can only pray He will, but you are asking too much of me as a simple human being – "

Galina spread out her hands in a little gesture.

"There is nothing to stop you from walking out and going back to the country and looking miserably at your house!"

Lord Bramton laughed.

"I love you when you are being sensible. Just as I love you whatever I hear you say. You are so perfect – the ideal I was quite certain can never exist in this world."

"Now you are frightening me," exclaimed Galina. "Perhaps it is a test and when you get to Ranmore House, you are disillusioned and you will only blame yourself for asking too much."

"I just adore everything about you, Galina. You are unique and because I feel as if an angel has been sent down from Heaven to guide me, I shall do exactly as you tell me to do."

Galina gave a little cry.

"That is unfair. If things go wrong, you will blame me rather than yourself."

"We will sink or swim together," he asserted, "and I promise that I will try not to embarrass you, but it will be difficult not to tell you how much I love you *all the time*."

"If we do that when we are alone, we must be very careful how we treat each other in public."

Galina was feeling that it would be a great mistake, when Georgie was away, for Mr. Farlow to think that she was having a wild flirtation with Lord Bramton.

More in the back of her mind was that she could not help but think that, with his enormous fortune, Mr. Farlow would help Lord Bramton.

Perhaps he could rent his house in the country for a month or so when the Season was over.

Perhaps he could offer him a position in one of the many new developments he was so interested in.

As one of the young Americans had said last night, he was constantly looking out for new inventions and new discoveries to make himself even richer.

As these ideas coursed through her mind, she was conscious that Lord Bramton knew what she was thinking.

She smiled at him.

"There is no need for us to speak. If you read my thoughts and I read yours, we could just sit in *silence*!"

"What you are thinking about is very practical and I promise that I will try not to disappoint you. Equally I am terrified you will find it boring to wait and will therefore marry someone else."

"I have no intention of marrying anyone, as I told Georgie the other day."

"Why ever not?"

"Because like you I shall wait for love," said Galina before she could stop herself.

He made a sound of triumph and then picked up her hand again.

"I love you, my darling."

As he spoke he was looking at her.

She felt her heart turn over in her breast.

Then Lord Bramton stated,

"Of course, I *do* love you. I shall do whatever you wish. I shall keep silent and behave with strict propriety until events develop in our favour."

He smiled before he added,

"Is that what you want me to say?"

"Of course it is, and now we must go back to the ballroom. We have been away for too long as it is."

"You are quite right," Lord Bramton admitted.

They stood up but for a moment they did not move.

Galina knew that he was longing with every nerve in his body to take her into his arms and kiss her.

But somehow he managed to control himself.

Then they walked back the way they had come.

As they saw ahead the fairy lights which decorated the park and the Chinese lanterns on the trees, he suddenly disappeared.

For a moment Galina could not understand why he had left her without saying anything.

Then she saw one of her admirers hurrying down the path towards her.

She moved quickly through the trees towards him.

"Oh, there you are, Lady Galina," he called. "This is our dance and I could not find you."

"I am so sorry," she replied. "But the garden is so beautiful in the moonlight that I forgot the time."

"I have already heard that the Duke prides himself on his garden – and the one at Woburn is famous."

"I hope one day I shall see it."

When she was finally back in the ballroom, Galina was relieved to see that Ellie-May was dancing.

Her partner was a good-looking young gentleman and he was obviously enjoying himself.

Galina saw the reproachful look on the face of the man who had gone to fetch her some lemonade and found she had disappeared when he had returned with it.

She smiled apologetically, but he then turned away without responding.

As she danced around the ballroom she was really thinking about Lord Bramton and all the amazingly strange yet wonderful words he had said to her.

'How can I possibly be in love with a man I had not seen until dinner-time tonight?' she protested to herself.

She reckoned that she was in love as she had never

before felt the puzzling feelings that seemed to be moving within her.

When she was taken into the supper room, she was seated at a small table with one of her dancing partners.

She saw Ellie-May come in with Lord Bramton and they sat down at a table with a number of other guests.

Galina realised that Ellie-May was laughing and so was Lord Bramton.

Just for a moment she had a feeling that she knew was jealousy sweep through her, and then she told herself he was being very sensible.

He was coming to stay, as she had asked him to do, at Ranmore House and it was tactful for him to be friendly with the daughter of his host.

Then something flashed through her mind.

Perhaps when he realised how very rich Mr. Farlow was and that Ellie-May would indeed inherit his enormous fortune, he would then change his mind and be practical and marry her.

Because the idea was disturbing, Galina rose to go back to the ballroom.

As she did so she passed the table where Ellie-May was sitting with Lord Bramton.

He looked up as she passed and their eyes met and just for a second or so they were invisibly joined together.

In that moment Galina knew that what he had said to her earlier was the *truth*.

It was wrong of her to doubt him.

He loved her and although it seemed impossible she in turn loved him.

Somehow by a miracle they had to find a way to be together in the future.

As she felt emotionally disturbed for the moment, Galina, instead of looking out for her partner, went towards Mr. Farlow.

He was busy talking to the Duke of Bedford in one of the rooms just off the ballroom.

As she joined them the Duke smiled at her and said,

"I am so glad your brother could be with us tonight. He tells me he has a horse running at Ascot which is sure to win, so I shall certainly back it."

"That is Swift Arrow," replied Galina, "and I think he has a very good chance."

"I have just been advising Mr. Farlow," added the Duke, "that he is extremely lucky to be staying at Ranmore House. I think it is one of the most attractive houses in London. My father used to tell me what magnificent balls your grandfather gave for your father when he appeared on the Social scene."

"I have heard about them too," smiled Galina.

"What I have heard," Mr. Farlow interposed, "has made me determined to give a ball for my daughter. And what could be more delightful than that it should take place at Ranmore House."

"I agree with you," came in the Duke, "and I only hope I shall receive an invitation."

"Of course you will, and I would be most grateful if you and your wife would be kind enough to give me a list of some of the young ladies here tonight who I could invite as my guests."

"We would be very pleased to help in any way we can and I hope we shall meet on other occasions when you can tell me more about the oil wells you have discovered in America, and your interest in other projects that I too am interested in."

"I shall be most delighted to do so, Your Grace," Mr. Farlow replied.

The Duke turned away to speak to another of his guests and Mr. Farlow then turned to address Galina with an expression of satisfaction in his eyes.

"I'm so very grateful to you for bringing Ellie-May and me here tonight and I think the Duke is an extremely charming man."

He did not say more and Galina was quite certain that he was thinking how the Duke could be an asset to him in business.

"Are you really going to give a ball?" she asked.

"I'll talk about it tomorrow morning, but as far as I'm concerned the sooner the better."

Galina paused and wondered if she ought to try to postpone the ball until Georgie had returned.

'I must speak to him about it,' she thought.

Then almost because she really needed him, he was walking towards her.

"Are you having a good time?" Georgie asked as he reached her.

"Mr. Farlow has just told the Duke that he intends to give a ball," Galina told him a little breathlessly. "And he wants to give it as soon as possible."

"I think that is a very good idea, but we must find out which nights are free when no one else will be having a ball or they will take all the best guests from us!"

Mr. Farlow laughed at this remark.

"I did not think of that."

"Most people go from ball to ball and it would be a mistake for you not to have the '*crème de la crème*'."

"I do agree with you," replied Mr. Farlow. "So we

must ask your secretary for some suitable dates first thing tomorrow morning."

"Galina will certainly help you," Georgie offered, "as I am afraid I have to be away for a few days."

Mr. Farlow raised his eyebrows.

"Where are you going? Back to the country?"

"Oh, no, nothing like that."

He looked over his shoulder as if someone might be listening and then he lowered his voice,

"The Secretary of State for Foreign Affairs has just asked me to slip over to France and do something for him. I am afraid I cannot tell you what it is, but it is so important that I cannot refuse to go."

Mr. Farlow was obviously impressed.

"I understand, of course I understand, my dear boy, and we will have the ball when you return."

"I am not quite certain when that will be, but fix a date while you have the chance and you can be sure I shall do my best to be with you."

Having said what he wanted to say, he would have walked away, but Galina put her hand on his arm.

"Listen, Georgie," she muttered so only he could hear. "I have asked Lord Bramton to stay because he is so hard up he cannot afford to go on staying at his Club."

"Oh, poor Victor, he really is in a state, of course, do what you can for him. Unless he marries Ellie-May, I cannot help feeling that he will have to close his beautiful house."

Galina was thinking that Lord Bramton might well marry Ellie-May as she herself had suggested.

If he did, she would lose something very precious which she did not want to lose.

The ball ended at one o'clock when the Duke told the band to play 'God Save the Queen'.

Galina had been ready to leave much earlier and yet she had not done so because Ellie-May was having such a marvellous time.

She obviously had many more partners than there were dances and gentlemen were buzzing around her like flies.

Lord Bramton must have disappeared fairly early as Galina could see no sign of him as they all lined up to say goodnight to their host and hostess.

"It's been a wonderful party. I did not know a ball could be so fabulous," Ellie-May gushed as she left.

"Much of its beauty was due to you," the Duke told her gallantly, "and I am looking forward to the ball your father is giving for you at Ranmore House."

Ellie-May gave a little cry.

"I've not heard about it yet. Oh, how exciting! I do hope Papa will invite all the charming people I've met tonight and that they will come."

The Duke laughed.

"I am sure they will if you invite them. And please don't forget I want an invitation too!"

"I promise we'll not forget you."

"Your Grace shall be the first guest we invite," Mr. Farlow added. "As yours is the first ball we have attended in London."

"It is something I should not dream of missing."

Then they had to move, as their host had a long line of guests waiting somewhat impatiently to say goodbye.

As they drove away, Georgie remarked,

"Well, you two girls were definitely the success of

60

tonight and I am sure that Mr. Farlow is as proud of you as I am."

"It was a lovely, lovely party," Ellie-May answered enthusiastically. "Two of my partners fought over me."

"I saw that," said her father, "and I thought that one seemed a very charming young gentleman."

"I cannot remember his name," admitted Ellie-May, "but he had a title of some sort and he paid me very many compliments which I enjoyed."

"You must try to remember his name," said Galina, "and we will ask him to your ball."

"I hope I'll meet him again before that. You said we have a party or a ball nearly every night and he told me he would look out for me at all of them."

"I see that I shall have to find out about this young man," Mr. Farlow came in. "I don't want you pursued by fortune-hunters. If he has not got a penny to bless himself with, we will kick him out the front door!"

Galina was now listening anxiously, as she did not want Mr. Farlow to be rude to Lord Bramton.

Perhaps he would think he was pursuing Ellie-May because he had come to stay in Ranmore House.

She therefore told Georgie again that his old friend was moving in.

"He says he is so uncomfortable at his Club that he would rather be with us. I know that Mr. Farlow will be interested in hearing what a wonderful house he owns."

"Wonderful is the right word," Georgie replied as he obviously realised what his sister was doing.

"In what way?" Mr. Farlow asked a little sharply.

"It is one of the oldest ancestral houses in England. In fact I have to admit the oldest. The pictures which have been collected over the years, just like the furniture, are all museum pieces.

"He also owns a collection of Greek statues, which one of his ancestors stole from Delos or one of the other islands when the Greeks could not protect themselves or their possessions."

"I would indeed like to see them," said Mr. Farlow.

"I know Victor would be delighted to show them to you and it only takes a day to drive to his house."

"You say he comes from a very old family?"

"A most distinguished family as it so happens. His grandmother was a Princess related to Princess Alexandra and his mother was the daughter of the Duke of Sussex."

Mr. Farlow was clearly impressed and Galina felt that he was turning over in his mind whether Lord Bramton would be a suitable husband for Ellie-May.

She could only pray as they drove on that he would help Lord Bramton.

At the same time she hoped he would not take any his patronage if he did not propose marriage.

She could now clearly see the difficulties over Lord Bramton if he came to stay at Ranmore House.

Yet she could not contain a feeling of excitement within herself because she would see him regularly and he would be near her.

It only took a short time to reach Park Lane.

When everyone had gone upstairs, Georgie came to Galina's room.

"Are you really leaving tomorrow?" she asked him.

"The sooner I can get on with this the better, and I understand Farlow has received a lot of telegrams since he arrived, but we do not know what is in them."

"How can we, Georgie?"

"I have given the butler his orders that, as there are strange people in the house and as we do not want letters and telegrams to be mixed up, everything has to be brought to you as soon as it arrives."

"That is indeed a sensible idea."

"It will give you a good chance to look through the telegrams before they are taken to Farlow and if you delay one or two while I am at sea, it will be very helpful."

"It would be terrible if he found out was what I was doing!" exclaimed Galina.

"Of course it would," her brother agreed, "but you are too sensible to take unnecessary risks."

"I just hope you are right, but you are asking a great deal of me and I only hope I shall not fail you."

"You have not failed me yet and we have had some good times together, old girl. We cannot throw it all away just because we have not got the money to keep it going."

"No, of course not," sighed Galina, "and you must take care of yourself. I suppose you are travelling under an assumed name."

"I managed to dig up a passport that was left behind a few years ago by a Johnson Donaldson, a friend of mine who died before I could return it. I have written down his name for you, so that you will not forget it."

"Is it wise for you to be so disguised?"

"It may be quite unnecessary. In which case I shall quickly become myself again. But what I do not want is one of Mr. Farlow's wild-catters to tell him I am asking questions or anything like that."

"Of course, you are so right, Georgie. If he had the slightest idea of what you were doing, he might walk out of here without paying his bills."

"I don't think he would do that, but we want him to stay where he is and give balls and parties at his expense, which will make life easier for me."

Galina knew he was thinking that some bills from Ranmore House had been overdue for a long time.

It was, however, just the same in the country, but she could not imagine how they could persuade Mr. Farlow to pay those.

As if she had spoken aloud her, brother added,

"If Mr. Farlow wants to go to the country and spend a weekend there, then encourage him as long as he pays for everything. Newland tells me he pays most bills that are put in front of him without even looking at them!"

Mr. Newland was the Earl's secretary who lived in a flat in the mews.

He was a middle-aged man who had never married and he was brilliant at handling all their money affairs even though he had to placate some angry shopkeepers and other institutions whose bills were long overdue.

She was certain, although she did not say so, that Mr. Newland would make Mr. Farlow pay for everything possible.

He would not miss anything that could in any way be attributed to the fact that he was staying in the house.

"I am leaving before breakfast," Georgie was now saying, "and I will telegraph you with my address as soon as I arrive."

"I only hope I shall remember all this and it will be rather difficult for me to avoid making a mistake."

"We cannot afford even one," he insisted, "and that is the truth."

He kissed Galina.

"Do take care of yourself, dearest, and for goodness

sake keep Farlow and Ellie-May in a good temper until I come back."

"I suppose that you are not thinking of marrying her yourself?"

"Actually tonight, after you had transformed her, I did think of it," admitted Georgie. "But quite frankly any girl of that age would bore me stiff in a fortnight and all the money in the world cannot sweep away boredom!"

Galina laughed.

"That is very true and when you do marry someone, I want you to be really in love with her."

"And I will say the same to you, Galina, but where you are concerned, you have to love his bank balance as well as him!"

As he finished speaking he kissed Galina again and walked to the door and as he opened it, he turned round,

"Goodnight and dream of the Shah of Persia at your feet!"

He did not wait for her reply, but walked down the passage to the Master suite.

It was as she undressed and got into bed that Galina found herself thinking not of the Shah of Persia but of Lord Bramton.

It was impossible to forget the strange and unusual emotion he awoke in her.

'I know I have made a mistake,' she whispered to herself, 'in asking him to stay here but how could I help it.'

She closed her eyes and she could still feel Lord Bramton kissing her hand.

CHAPTER FOUR

The invitations to parties, balls and other forms of entertainment were pouring in.

It was clear that the Social world was amused and fascinated by Mr. Farlow and his daughter.

In the next few days Galina never had a moment to herself.

She was either discussing the invitations with Ellie-May or deciding what she should wear and then they were rushing off to the shops or hurrying even faster back as so many people were calling to see them.

As Mr. Farlow had some business acquaintances in London, he was as busy as they were.

It occurred to Galina that the great house which had always seemed to be so gloomy whenever she and Georgie were alone had now become almost like a parrot's cage.

Everyone seemed to be talking at the same time, running down corridors or trying to find her.

If she went upstairs to rest, there was certain to be a message or an unexpected visitor.

Galina was kept so busy that she did not worry, as she had expected to do, about Georgie.

She did not even worry too much when there were no telegrams from America for Mr. Farlow.

She had expected, from what Georgie had told her, that he would be having one every other day and then she would have to detain them until she could telegraph their contents to Georgie.

Nothing happened, but she hardly had time to think about it.

She was, however, vividly conscious and at times very grateful that Lord Bramton was with them.

He proved a tower of strength when people arrived unexpectedly. This had often happened and when Galina could not be found, he had to take her place.

Lord Bramton talked to everyone and showed them the Picture Gallery and all the other rooms where there was some particular collection that would interest them.

"I just don't know what I would do without you," Galina told him one day.

He had coped with a group of Americans who had just arrived in England and who were determined to make themselves known to Mr. Farlow.

"I just hope you will never have to handle all these people yourself," Lord Bramton said to her very quietly.

As Galina looked up at him she knew that was what she was hoping herself.

Only when she had left him, did she say to herself,

'It is *impossible* – impossible! I am only making it worse by depending on him and feeling as I do when he is near me.'

*

It was not until the beginning of the following week that a telegram arrived addressed to Mr. Farlow.

As soon as Galina saw it in the basket amongst the letters that had been brought to her, she drew in her breath and felt afraid.

Now she would have to be very clever not to make

any mistakes and remember exactly what Georgie had told her to do.

She opened the telegram and found a brief message,

"*Have found a comfortable accommodation as you suggested in Titusville.*

Sam."

Galina read it through twice and then she went to the library.

She found a book on America and turned quickly to the chapter on Pennsylvania and was not surprised to learn that Titusville was a small town in the State.

Now she had the information that Georgie wanted.

But she had not yet heard from him and there was nothing she could do until she did.

Then she remembered him instructing her that the longer she could delay the telegram the better.

It seemed such a wrong thing to do to anyone.

Yet if another well had been found for Mr. Farlow, it could not hurt him so very much if he was three or four days delayed in drilling for it.

At the same time, feeling uncomfortable and rather ashamed of herself, Galina slipped the telegram into one of the drawers of her writing desk.

She was praying that Georgie was not losing a good chance of finding an oil well as it would save them from what she was more and more convinced was destruction.

Mr. Newland had told her only yesterday that the bank was complaining they were so overdrawn.

The money that Mr. Farlow was paying for renting Ranmore House was not enough to pay all the bills which had accumulated at Ranmore Park.

That night after she had retired to her bedroom, she drew the curtains back from the window.

She looked up at the moon and it seemed strange to think that the same moon was perhaps shining on Georgie.

Or it might be a sunny day in Pennsylvania and he was roving around the oil fields.

Wherever he was, she sent up a little prayer that he would soon let her know what he was doing.

She could then tell him that there was at least one possibility of an oil field.

Two days later she at last received a telegram. She opened it at once and when she saw the name 'Donaldson' she wanted to cry out with excitement.

He was there.

He was in America.

Now she would be able to get in touch with him.

To her astonishment she read,

"*Am staying at 48 Fifth Avenue for a few days, so let me know how you are.*

Donaldson."

Galina knew very little about America and yet she recognised that Fifth Avenue was the '*crème de la crème*' of New York where millionaires had their opulent houses.

'What on earth could Georgie be doing there?' she wondered. 'If nothing else, how can he afford it?'

However, she now had an address for him and she then sent him Mr. Farlow's telegram.

She had no idea what could be happening.

Because she was so worried and she had to confide in someone, she asked one of the footmen to inform Lord Bramton that she wished to see him.

He joined her in a few minutes and when he saw that she was alone, he closed the door firmly behind him.

Galina jumped up from where she had been sitting and ran towards him.

"I had to tell you, Victor, that I have had a telegram from Georgie and where do you think he is?"

"In America," he replied immediately.

As he spoke, she remembered that she had not told him where Georgie was going.

She supposed that he must have guessed or perhaps once again he was reading her thoughts!

But there was no reason to argue about that now.

"He is in Fifth Avenue. Can you believe it? What is he doing there?"

Lord Bramton pulled her gently onto the sofa and then he sat down beside her saying,

"Now, you are not to worry. If I know anything of Georgie, he is well capable of making himself comfortable and at ease wherever he is. I can assure you Fifth Avenue is extremely comfortable if rather too much so."

"Why is he there?" asked Galina.

"I rather think he is sensible enough to realise that is just where the gold of America is more easily found than anywhere else."

He saw the expression on Galina's face.

"I know he is not seeking gold, but knowing him, he is doing it in the most comfortable way and will perhaps succeed quicker than you expect."

"I don't understand. I did not mean you to know what Georgie is doing."

"I did not believe all that nonsense about going to France at the request of the Secretary of State for Foreign Affairs and because he has a good brain, I am quite certain he will come back with the goods."

"Oh, Victor, I do hope you are right. But it worries me *so* much."

"I will not allow you to worry, Galina. Everything is going so well at the moment and Mr. Farlow is delighted with himself and the impression he is making on London.

"I know he is going to ask you sooner or later, if he can hold a party at Ranmore Park and you will find that very advantageous."

"It will please Mr. Newland. He is worried about the expenses there which are mounting up and up."

"Just like mine are," sighed Lord Bramton.

Galina put out her hand and laid it on his arm.

"I am sorry. I keep worrying you with my troubles when you have terrible ones of your own."

"There I have to agree with you, Galina."

"I have not forgotten about you, Victor, and I have been praying that something will happen which will help you, but I have to think of Georgie first."

"Of course you do and I know, my darling one, if anyone's prayers will be heard, they will be yours."

He looked at her in a way which made Galina jump up from the sofa.

"Now, I must really get back to work, but you do think that Georgie is all right and there is nothing wrong or mysterious about him being in Fifth Avenue?"

"If I had any money, I would risk it all on betting that whatever Georgie is doing, it will be very much to his advantage!"

"That is exactly what I really want to hear, Victor, and now I am not so frightened."

"I will not allow you to be frightened of anything if I can prevent it," asserted Lord Bramton. "Can I tell you how lovely you are? You are more beautiful every time I look at you."

"I only wish it was true – "

"It is true and my lovely, my precious one, go on praying that by some miracle you and I can be together for always."

There was no need for Galina to answer him.

She just looked at him.

As their eyes met, she knew the only happiness for either of them would be if they could be together without the horror of their endless debts keeping them apart.

She turned back towards her writing desk and was wondering again what Georgie was doing in Fifth Avenue and if by a miracle he had found a way of making money.

What she did not know was something important had happened that would sweep away all her fears.

*

Georgie had, once again, fallen on his feet.

When he had climbed aboard the steamer to carry him off to New York, he had, against his better judgement, taken a First Class cabin.

He had seen some of the Second Class passengers going aboard and he sensed instinctively they would be of no use to him.

The First Class passengers were very different.

There was a good number of middle-aged men who looked rich and prosperous and the women accompanying them were well-dressed and bejewelled and that, if nothing else, told him their husbands' pockets were not at all like his own.

He had therefore taken a First Class cabin and when the ship was well underway, he had deliberately made the acquaintance of his fellow travellers.

He was aware that unlike the English, Americans were always prepared to be friendly to strangers.

He was soon chatting away with older men who he was quite certain in their own words were 'in the money'.

When they met up again before dinner in the bar, he accepted a drink from a man with white hair.

He seemed a little older than the others and had a better glass of champagne in front of him.

"Would you care to join me, Mr. Donaldson?" he asked.

Georgie had not hesitated.

"That is most kind of you, sir. It is something I would much appreciate at the moment."

"Then help yourself and please tell me why you are coming to my country?"

Georgie had been frank.

"I think you might guess the reason and I can only say, sir, I think that America is now the land of opportunity for young men like myself."

The American was pleased.

"You are quite right, and the more young men we encourage the better."

Georgie had to be very careful what he said about himself.

Mr. Wilbur was extremely rich and what was more he had already made a fortune in oil.

He could therefore tell Georgie what he wanted to know and explain how he had become such a success.

Mr. Wilbur, who so obviously liked to talk when he had an audience, was only too ready to tell Georgie what he wanted to know.

He told him how for some centuries Pennsylvanian farmers had found their streams muddied up by a sort of black glue. They cursed it and then following a tip from the Indians, they bottled it and sold it as a medicine.

"A medicine!" exclaimed Georgie. "I would never have thought of that."

"It was sold as a cure for asthma, rheumatism, gout, tuberculosis, cancer and fallen arches!"

"I can hardly believe it."

"It's true," replied Mr. Wilbur. "And what is more at the time of the Revolutionary War it was a sure remedy for constipation."

Georgie found all this very amusing.

"Then," Mr. Wilbur continued, "a certain Mr. Kier discovered it made a good if rather smelly lighting fluid. And that of course was just the beginning."

"It is more fascinating than a fairy story," Georgie said. "Please go on."

"I think it was in 1857, the owner of a small piece of land decided that underground an oil creek there must be a primary source for the substance Mr. Kier had bottled so profitably. He found that by tapping wells with a pick and shovel there was an ooze of oil."

Georgie was listening to him intently.

"When a friend of his nearly drowned," Mr. Wilbur continued, "because an underground spring erupted and he concluded, and was right, that oil lies deeper than water."

Georgie was entranced as Mr. Wilbur went on and described how a local blacksmith who was used to digging salt wells was persuaded to sink a seventy foot shaft.

On one sultry day in August the black glue bubbled up into a flood.

The same blacksmith was so excited he jumped on his mule and rode into Titusville crying, "struck oil, struck oil!"

Mr. Wilbur paused before he added,

"He had, in fact, hit on the first oil well."

"It is such an exciting story," enthused Georgie.

"As you can well imagine," Mr. Wilbur expanded his tale, "a great number of people and that included me, descended on Titusville with shovels and drills. Oil towns began to spring up around it like weeds."

"And that is how you made your millions."

"I did, and it was the most precious moment in my life when I could pay the proceeds of my first well into my bank."

He chuckled.

"Now, of course, all my friends are looking for oil in other places. But Titusville was the first and now there is a huge demand for oil which we never expected.

"It always amuses me to remember the year after John Drake's strike, a group of men in Cleveland sent John Rockefeller over to Oil Creek to report on the long range possibilities of the gushers."

"And what did he say?"

"After his first survey, he reported that oil had no commercial future."

"I don't believe it!"

"It's true, but he had to eat his words and it was a Rockefeller who guessed that oil might be used for heating and steamships."

"And of course he was right."

"Rockefeller and his partner pooled all their savings and invested just four thousand dollars in a candle-makers' refinery.

"Rockefeller became extremely rich and men are now building more refineries and getting richer every day. No one knows where it will all end.

"But now my guess is that this is just the beginning

of what oil can perform and there are a great many more discoveries ahead of us."

"That is just what I want to find out," Georgie said a little rashly.

"Well, I certainly can give you a hand," Mr. Wilbur told him as they journeyed across the Atlantic.

Georgie knew he had already struck gold.

He learnt quite a lot about Mr. Wilbur.

He married when he was very young as he wanted a girl with money and then she had run away with his best friend after three years of a rather unhappy marriage.

"We just weren't suited to each other," Mr. Wilbur told Georgie. "And you take my advice, young man, and don't marry anyone until you're real certain she'll listen to what you say. Also give you a son to whom you can leave your fortune once you've made it."

"Have you no children?"

Mr. Wilbur shook his head.

"No. When my wife left me, I decided I wouldn't marry again, but travel all over the world alone. It's been interesting, it's been exciting and I've had some real pretty women in my arms, but not for keeps. I enjoy travelling and no woman wants the discomfort of that."

"I can that see you are more than comfortable at the moment," remarked Georgie.

Mr. Wilbur laughed.

"Now I can travel First Class, be waited on hand and foot and buy the best champagne. But then I've done it the hard way and, I can tell you, that you can be damned uncomfortable and extremely rough!"

Georgie was fascinated by the stories Mr. Wilbur told him.

He listened attentively and he gathered the oil still brought him more money than anything else he had been interested in.

They often talked till they were the last passengers to retire to their cabins and they were talking again the next morning when they met at breakfast.

When the ship was ready to dock at the Port of New York, Georgie asked for Mr. Wilbur's advice on the easiest and quickest way to travel to the oil fields in Pennsylvania.

"If that's where you want to go, I'll take you there myself. It's very different to what it was when I went there first and you need to be so careful who you associate with.

"Those who are green know nothing about what's going on and usually find themselves lying in a ditch with every penny they ever possessed snatched from them!"

"I surely don't want that to happen to me!"

"I'll take you there," he offered, "and you'll learn more in one day with me and my wild-catters than you'll ever learn in three years with them, as they will think you are a greenhorn."

Georgie could see the commonsense of this advice and he was only too glad to accept Mr. Wilbur's invitation, but first he wanted to go to his house in Fifth Avenue.

When Georgie accompanied him there he found the telegram that Galina had sent to him.

It seemed like a miracle that she should be telling him that Mr. Farlow's spies had found oil in Titusville.

That was where Mr. Wilbur was going to take him.

Before they actually reached Fifth Avenue, Georgie learnt something new.

Some years ago when he was fifteen, an American boy called Thomas Edison became a telegraph operator.

"He was always," related Mr. Wilbur, "wanting to

take things apart and see how they worked. Then he would put them all together again and make them tick longer and louder at half the price. When he was nineteen he invented an electric vote recorder and two years later was working on a new fangled thing called a telephone."

"A *telephone*! How could he think of anything as clever as that? I have read about them, but I have never seen one."

"I've one myself," Mr. Wilbur boasted, "and there are one or two other products that are new and which I am considering putting some money into. I think they will be of interest to you."

"And what is Mr. Edison working on now?" asked Georgie rather breathlessly.

He had now begun to appreciate that Mr. Wilbur's mind jumped from one subject to another and, although he was so much younger, he was finding it hard to keep up with him.

"Well, I only saw him just before I went away and he is thinking of a new form of lighting."

"Lighting!" echoed Georgie.

"As you know most of us have gas, but Edison has told me that what he wants to find is a cheap filament so that the ordinary householder can have electric light."

"I can hardly believe it," sighed Georgie.

"Well, I do believe him and when you talk to him, you'll find yourself believing him too."

He paused before continuing,

"He has already had some success, but it's not good enough. You mark my words, my boy, electric light will very soon be in use in all the fashionable houses if they can afford it."

Georgie considered that he must be exaggerating.

Equally he had so often considered there were new ideas and new inventions in America that he could not find anywhere else.

'This is now a golden age for this country,' he told himself, 'and I would be a fool if I did not get in on it in some way.'

When they went to bed that night, Mr. Wilbur put a hand on Georgie's shoulder.

"You are just the sort of son I would have liked to have had. You're inquisitive and I believe in your mind you're saying, 'off with the old and on with the new' and that is what I've said all my life. Now just tell me what you want for the future."

Georgie laughed.

"That is quite easy, I want to be a millionaire like you!"

"Very well, that is what you *shall* be. Tomorrow we'll meet some of those who are thinking out new ideas which need my money to support them."

He smiled and added,

"You'll advise me when I should spend and when I should keep my pocket closed. Two brains are better than one and there are a great number of charlatans about who make fools of those who listen to what they say."

"I think they exist everywhere."

"You're quite right," replied Mr Wilbur, "and that is why I've had to learn to be so careful. Not only because I might lose money, but I might be made a fool of."

"We all hate that, but very unlike you, Mr. Wilbur, I cannot afford to lose money – even a small amount."

"We'll be careful that you don't take any risks. It's good for you to see what other men are planning and that is what I'm going to show you."

Georgie told him that he was more grateful than he could put into words.

Mr. Wilbur laughed.

"To tell the truth. I'm usually exceedingly bored with crossing the Atlantic, but I have enjoyed this last trip more than any other, because you are with me. I'm a man who pays my debts and I'm grateful to you for passing the time with me and I'm going to see you go back to England with your pockets filled."

He did not listen to Georgie's grateful thanks, but merely promised,

"Go to bed, my boy, and tomorrow we're going to strike oil in a number of different ways!"

"I would be content with just one way!"

"Don't you believe it. You reach out your hand whenever you have the chance and you may pick up a hot potato or a handful of gold. It's just chance and having, as they always said about me, 'the luck of the devil'!"

"That is just what I want!" cried Georgie.

As he got into bed, he thought that Galina would hardly believe when he told her that this conversation had really taken place.

*

While Georgie was asleep, as it happened, his sister was also having a great surprise.

She was writing her letter of thanks to the hostess who had entertained her last night and being effusive as it was always polite to do so.

Actually she had thought it had been a dull ball, but perhaps she was prejudiced.

She had hoped and indeed longed for Lord Bramton to dance a waltz with her.

But to her surprise he danced with everyone else in their party including, of course, Ellie-May and then he had danced with several of the other pretty girls they had met on previous occasions.

When finally the dancing was almost over, he had asked Galina for a dance.

Rather petulantly she pouted,

"I thought you had forgotten about me."

He took her hand and drew her onto the floor.

"I am looking after your reputation, as your brother would want me to do, if he was here."

"But I wanted to dance with you," Galina said like a small child.

"And I wanted to dance with you. It is the nearest I can get to Heaven to have my arm around you and feel you close against me."

He spoke with such a sincere note in his voice that Galina felt a little thrill run through her.

She knew now why the ball had seemed so dull – it was simply because she was bored with everyone she was dancing with.

She only wanted to be with Victor.

He did not speak while they danced, but she knew he was enjoying every moment they were on the floor.

As the waltz they were dancing was very romantic, it seemed to Galina as if they had stepped into a fairyland together and everything was so exquisite.

As the dance came to an end, Lord Bramton said,

"Now I am going to leave you, as I will not have you talked about. You know, as well as I do, that you are far too beautiful not to have every other girl of your age jealous of you and their mothers willing to make trouble."

Lord Bramton moved away as someone came up to speak to her.

She felt almost as if she had lost him.

Now as she heard the door of the sitting room open, she looked up expectedly hoping it was him.

It was the butler who announced,

"Sir Christopher Lawson to see you, my Lady."

Galina looked round in surprise.

She had been introduced to Sir Christopher once at a dinner party and she knew he was an *aide-de-camp* to the Prince of Wales.

Sir Christopher, a good-looking young gentleman of about twenty-seven, smiled as he came towards her.

"I came, Lady Galina," he said, "to see your brother but I understand that he is abroad."

"He is in France and he will be sorry to miss you."

"I am sorry too," replied Sir Christopher, "as I have an invitation for him and you and your house party from His Royal Highness, the Prince of Wales."

Galina's eyes opened wide in surprise.

"An invitation," she echoed and then remembering her manners, she suggested, "please will you sit down."

They sat down in armchairs.

"If it is an invitation to Marlborough House, I know that Georgie will be very disappointed he is not here."

"Actually," responded Sir Christopher, "His Royal Highness would be very pleased if you and Mr. Farlow and his daughter would spend this next Friday to Monday at Sandringham."

Galina gave a little gasp.

"*Sandringham?*" she queried.

"Their Royal Highnesses decided that they would go to Sandringham because on Saturday afternoon Princess Alexandra is opening the local Flower Show. His Royal Highness thought you may enjoy seeing the house and the garden which is very beautiful at this time of the year."

Sir Christopher gave a little laugh before he added,

"I think there are more daffodils than in any other garden in England and at present they are at their best."

"I would love to see them," enthused Galina, "and it is so very kind of Their Royal Highnesses to invite Mr. Farlow and his daughter as well."

Sir Christopher smiled.

"His Royal Highness has been interested in all the stories he has heard about Mr. Farlow and how enormously rich he is and I suppose the tale is somewhat exaggerated."

"On the contrary, I think Mr. Farlow is even richer than the tales about him and it is all due to *oil*."

"I have heard about the oil which is being obtained in America and I think I ought to go out there and inspect it for myself."

With some difficulty Galina prevented herself from telling him that was exactly what Georgie was doing.

Instead she suggested,

"As my brother is away, Lord Bramton, who I am sure you know, has been helping me entertain Mr. Farlow. As his house is not far from Sandringham, I wonder if it would be possible for him to come with us. I am sure His Royal Highness would like to see the amazing treasures that I hear are in Bramton Priory."

"I have heard of them too and I have often thought that it would be easy to reach the Priory from Sandringham, but the opportunity has never occurred."

There was silence and then Galina looked at him questioningly.

"Speaking off the cuff," said Sir Christopher, "I am sure that His Royal Highness would be delighted for Lord Bramton to be in your party. Perhaps we could go over to the Priory on Sunday after Church."

"I am certain that Lord Bramton would be only too pleased to arrange it, but he would not like to think that he had pushed himself onto His Royal Highness."

"I think the issue is, Lady Galina, that His Royal Highness would be a bit put out at having to find another man as your brother is away and it would be far easier to tell him that the figures are correct for the weekend party."

Galina laughed out loud as it sounded so funny, but she guessed that once the Prince of Wales had made up his mind about something, he was exceedingly annoyed if his plans were upset in any way.

"I was not expecting such an exciting and unusual invitation and you must tell us exactly what time to arrive and I hope I do not make any silly mistakes."

"If you do it will be my fault," Sir Christopher said gallantly, "and we look forward to your arrival on Friday."

He rose to his feet as he spoke and Galina added,

"There is one thing I would like to say to you, but please promise you will not tell anyone what I have said."

"No, of course not."

She knew that Sir Christopher was rather surprised and curious as to what she was going to say.

"I do not think many people know it," Galina began a little nervously, "but Lord Bramton is finding it difficult to make both ends meet. He is actually thinking of having to close his house."

Sir Christopher gave an exclamation.

"That would be a real disaster. It is one of the most famous houses in England."

"Yes, I know, but houses like his cost so much and Lord Bramton is wondering how he can survive."

Sir Christopher did not speak and she continued,

"I have heard that His Royal Highness is very fond of gambling. Can you make it clear that it is impossible for Lord Bramton to sit down at a card table?"

"I understand, of course, I do understand. I am so grateful to you, Lady Galina, for telling me. I will see that the numbers at the table are correct and find something for Lord Bramton to do."

"That is very very kind of you."

She thought as she spoke that he was not only a charming young man but a very handsome one.

Vaguely at the back of her mind she had the idea he was quite well off.

He had been in the Household Brigade before the Prince of Wales had asked him to become one of his *aides-de-camp*.

It was so annoying that Georgie was not here to tell her everything she wanted to know, but she expected she could find out a little more from her relatives.

It was also a great pity that Georgie was away as he would have enjoyed going to Sandringham.

The Prince of Wales might have helped in some way over Ranmore Park.

Then she told herself she was being absurd.

There was only one person who really could help them and that was Mr. Farlow.

She was sure now that Mr. Farlow and Ellie-May would be thrilled at the chance of going to Sandringham –

they would certainly have something to boast about when they returned to New York.

She walked into the hall with Sir Christopher.

"Is it going to be a big party?"

Sir Christopher shrugged his shoulders.

"One never knows with His Royal Highness. He is quite capable of asking enough people at the last moment to fill the Albert Hall, or alternatively he wants just a few cosy evenings with guests who interest him."

"I can see your position is a rather difficult one."

"Fortunately I have a lot of help, but frankly I am enjoying it, because it is never monotonous and one never fails to be surprised when one least expects it."

Galina laughed and as she did so, Ellie-May came down the stairs.

She had been shopping earlier in the afternoon and she had gone upstairs to tidy herself before tea.

"Oh, here comes Miss Farlow now," Galina told Sir Christopher. "We are just going to have tea. Please stay and have a cup with us."

"I ought to get back to Marlborough House, but, of course, I could say that you delayed me!"

As Ellie-May reached the last step, Galina said,

"I want to introduce you to Sir Christopher Lawson who has brought you and your father the most delightful invitation."

Ellie-May put out her hand.

"That sounds fun. What is it?"

"To spend Friday to Monday at Sandringham with their Royal Highnesses, the Prince and Princess of Wales."

Ellie-May looked at Galina.

"I don't believe it – you are pulling my leg."

"No, it is true," came in Sir Christopher, "and I am delighted to meet you, Miss Farlow. Everyone has told His Royal Highness how attractive you are, and he is looking forward to welcoming you as his guest."

"Then it is true, really true!" cried Ellie-May.

As Sir Christopher nodded, she laughed,

"Papa will be over the moon. As we don't have Royalty in America, it is one of those things he would like to collect and show off to everyone else."

The way she said it was so naïve, Sir Christopher almost burst out laughing.

They walked towards the sitting room where their tea was waiting for them.

As they did so, Galina was aware that Mr. Farlow would think that whatever his visit to England cost him, it would be well worth every penny now.

CHAPTER FIVE

As Ellie-May had forecast her father was 'over the moon' when told they had been invited to Sandringham.

At first he, too, thought it was a joke.

Then he was as excited as a schoolboy at what lay ahead of them.

He insisted the next morning that Galina and Ellie-May went shopping again and bought more new dresses.

"We really have enough that have cost you a lot of money already," Galina told him.

"Money! What is money?" Mr. Farlow answered. "I want both Ellie-May and you to look your very best and I've never yet known a woman refuse a new dress!"

Galina laughed.

"I have not had the opportunity to refuse many and thank you very much indeed."

They went to the same shop they had been to before because they knew Ellie-May's fitting.

The vendeuse found what Galina believed was the prettiest gown ever designed and it made Ellie-May look really glamorous or as she would say, 'a million dollars'.

Galina knew that her father would be proud of her.

She only wished that Georgie was going with them, and she could not help thinking that in some way the visit to Sandringham would be of benefit to Lord Bramton.

He was very surprised by the invitation and asked at once,

"Did you ask for me to come with you?"

"Of course I did, Victor, and Sir Christopher was so relieved as otherwise we would have been a man short on His Royal Highness's calculations."

"Well, I am delighted to be included in the party, I have not been to Sandringham for a long time and I know you will enjoy seeing it."

"What I am hoping," said Galina, "is that, as I have already suggested to Sir Christopher, we could go over with His Royal Highness to see your house on Sunday."

Lord Bramton stared at her.

"You don't mean it?"

"Well, I want to see it for one thing and I am sure it will interest the Prince of Wales as he is so fond of seeing places he has not already visited."

"I am glad you warned me. I must be in touch with my caretakers immediately and order them to open up the rooms, pull back the curtains and air the whole house."

"I tell you what we will do," suggested Galina. "I will arrange for one of the servants to go there tomorrow and warn them. It will be better than writing a letter which doubtless they will be unable to read."

"It is asking too much of you – "

"I don't think there is any point in my mentioning that Mr. Farlow will be paying for the conveyance!"

Lord Bramton laughed, but because she could read his thoughts, Galina realised that actually he disliked being beholden to anyone.

Their instructions from Sir Christopher arrived in plenty of time.

A special coach was reserved on the train from St. Pancras to Wolferton which was the nearest station.

"I am only surprised," Mr. Farlow surmised, when he was informed about the arrangements, "that His Royal Highness does not have a train of his own."

"Then you must suggest it to him," said Galina. "It would look very smart in Royal colours with every carriage flying a Union Jack!"

"I think Royalty should look like Royalty. If I had my way they would wear their crowns every day!"

They all laughed at his grand ideas, but Galina was delighted he was so pleased with the invitation.

*

They set off after luncheon and drove to the station in a comfortable carriage drawn by two horses.

Behind them came two lady's maids and two men-servants to be valets to Mr. Farlow and Lord Bramton.

Ellie-May was thrilled with the special coach and she explored it the moment they were shown into it by the Station Master.

It was upholstered in a Royal red and all the chairs were most comfortable.

There were two Stewards on board to provide them with drinks ranging from coffee to champagne as well as delicious *pâté* sandwiches.

"Now this is real luxury," Mr. Farlow commented, "and if I am born again I hope I shall come back as a Royal personage."

"I am sure that is what you are already in America," added Galina. "When they hear where you have been staying I am certain that your friends will curtsy and bow to you!"

She was teasing, but she had the feeling that he was taking it all seriously.

They all chatted and laughed as they journeyed from London through the countryside.

Galina was very conscious that Lord Bramton was sitting beside her.

He did not say very much and yet she knew that his eyes were watching her.

Occasionally when they looked at each other, they forgot what they were saying.

When they arrived at Wolferton Station, they found the Royal carriages waiting for them.

It was not a very long drive and when Galina had her first sight of Sandringham, she exclaimed in delight.

The house was as attractive as she had expected it to be and, as they were moving up the drive, she had her first glimpse of all the golden daffodils that Sir Christopher had promised her. They were even more profuse than she could possibly have imagined.

They bordered all the lawns and lakes and made the trees appear to be standing on golden carpets.

They drew up outside the enormous house with its turrets, towers and long high chimneys.

Galina had already learnt from Lord Bramton that the house had been mentioned in the Doomsday Book as St. Deringham, the name of the village nearby.

Actually the present house was built in the second half of the eighteenth century by Charles Spencer Cooper, but he had died before it was completed.

The Prince of Wales rebuilt the main house some years later and Galina was told when she was going round Sandringham that His Royal Highness had preserved the original conservatory and made it into a billiard room.

As she entered the house she recognised that it was as exciting for her as well as Ellie-May and she was certain that for Mr. Farlow it was as good as passing through the gates of Paradise.

The Prince and Princess were waiting to greet them and as was usual the Prince put everyone at their ease.

No one, Galina thought, could have looked more attractive than the Princess of Wales.

They were offered tea in a room that was rather like those at Marlborough House – it seemed to be somewhat over-furnished and contain more dogs than Galina had ever seen in a private house.

It was when they went upstairs to dress for dinner that Galina told Ellie-May she must, on no account, be late.

She had heard when her friends were talking about the Prince of Wales that he was a stickler for punctuality.

"You will hardly believe it," one woman had said at a party, "but all the Sandringham clocks are kept half-an-hour fast!"

Everyone had laughed at this, but Galina was even more determined that no one in her party should upset His Royal Highness.

Actually she was to learn later that a great deal of his frustrated energy – because, his mother, Queen Victoria would not allow him to take any part in ruling the country – went in planning his parties.

He actually chose the room for each guest and gave directions for the clothes he expected everyone to wear at each meal.

Lord Bramton knew about this scenario and he had said to Mr. Farlow in the train,

"Nothing, I am confidentially told, can annoy His Royal Highness more than to see Orders incorrectly worn or a black waistcoat when a white one should be worn."

"I only hope I shall not make any mistakes, Victor. You did tell me yesterday that my clothes are all correct."

"Indeed they are," confirmed Lord Bramton, who in

Georgie's absence had taken Mr. Farlow to the best tailor in Mayfair.

Because they arrived in time for tea, Galina noticed that the Princess was wearing an ordinary day dress.

She had been informed that the Prince expected the ladies at tea-time to dress up for the occasion.

"They should all look just like butterflies," she was told, "in elaborately flowing tea-gowns of chiffon, lace or fur trimmed velvet."

She felt glad that Mr. Farlow had insisted on them buying new clothes and indeed it was Ellie-May who had insisted on having not two evening dresses but five.

"Do I look all right?" Ellie-May asked when she came into Galina's bedroom.

"You look lovely, dear Ellie-May," replied Galina.

It was certainly the truth.

When Ellie-May was feeling animated and her hair was beautifully arranged, she looked like a fairy Princess.

Galina was quite certain, although she did not say so, that everyone saw her with a golden cloud of sparkling dollars around her.

They walked downstairs together and were taken to an ornate reception room.

There were tall glasses of champagne being handed round by powdered footmen and then they were gradually joined by the other members of the house party.

They were all more elderly than Galina and Ellie-May, but Sir Christopher and Lord Bramton were there to keep them amused.

Dinner was at half-past eight, but as Sir Christopher had told them, the guests were expected to be downstairs at eight o'clock prompt to await the arrival of the Prince and Princess.

This gave Galina time to meet the other guests and they were all as Lord Bramton whispered to her,

"Laced and high-boned, fringed and flounced and glittering with every jewel they possessed."

The latter was not quite true, but there was certainly a great display of jewellery.

Galina was so grateful to Lord Bramton for telling her that long gloves were always worn.

"At dinner!" she had exclaimed.

Lord Bramton nodded.

"It seems strange, but that is His Royal Highness's orders. You take them off at dinner and put them on again afterwards."

"Personally I think it's ridiculous!"

"You may think so, Galina."

Lord Bramton had stayed at Sandringham six years ago with his parents and fortunately he remembered what was expected.

Because he was so knowledgeable he had prevented Galina making unfortunate mistakes and being too worried about what she should do and not do.

Mr. Farlow and Ellie-May listened most attentively to everything they were told.

They did not even criticise or laugh at what Galina thought was almost exaggerated protocol.

"Precedence," Lord Bramton told them, "is one of the Prince's favourite hobby horses. You will see that we go into dinner precisely according to our rank."

This meant, Galina knew, that Mr. Farlow and his daughter would be among the last and she only hoped they would not feel hurt.

As they waited before dinner, she had an idea that most of the guests were keeping their eye on the door.

When their host and hostess arrived the men bowed and the women swept to the floor in a deep curtsy.

Then the Princess led the way to the dining room on the arm of the gentleman of the highest rank.

Galina could not help thinking that if Georgie had been there, it would have been him.

The Princess was followed by the Prince with the most distinguished lady present, who was, Galina thought, exceedingly lovely.

She was to learn later that she was the Countess of Warwick with whom His Royal Highness was enamoured at the moment.

To her great delight Galina found that her partner at dinner was Lord Bramton.

"I am very glad it's you," she whispered, as he held out his arm to her.

"I have won the position," he replied with a twinkle in his eyes, "by exactly twenty-five years. I am certain that our host looked me up in Debrett's before he was sure."

Galina giggled and then she remarked,

"We must behave properly and you must prevent me from making any social *faux pas*."

"You will not make any, Galena, and if you do, no one could help but forgive you, because you are so lovely."

The way he spoke made Galina feel a little quiver surge through her.

Just for a second, because she could not help it, her fingers tightened on his arm.

The dinner was delicious and this, she had already learnt, was because the Prince had a very large appetite.

"In fact," Lord Bramton had told her earlier, "a new dish that is delicious puts him in a better humour than the wittiest response from one of his pretty ladies!"

"Do tell me more about him," Galina had begged.

"You will find out most things for yourself, as it is some years since I have been at Sandringham. But then I have been asked to Marlborough House and everyone talks so much about the Prince of Wales. He is undoubtedly the most interesting gentleman in England at present – "

He paused before he had added,

"Although I daresay any number of people would disagree with me."

"What you tell me I have to repeat, if it is suitable, to Mr. Farlow and Ellie-May, so what should I know?"

Lord Bramton chuckled, but he did tell her that the Prince was an unexpectedly good listener rather than going on chatting about himself.

Therefore it was important to think of conversation to amuse him before you were actually sitting at his side.

"The most ominous sign when he is bored," Lord Bramton elaborated, "is that his fingers begin to fidget with the cutlery and his eyes stray along the table. My mother once said that if he murmured – 'quite so! quite so!' you knew you had failed. He was bored and hoping the meal would soon end!"

"You are making me frightened and now I wish we were not going," Galina had exclaimed.

"You know that is not true," he had answered. "I am delighted to go to Sandringham again simply because I am going with you"

"I shall feel exactly like going to school for the first time. You promise that you will keep near me and prevent me from making some terrible *faux pas*."

"You know I want to be near you, my Galina."

He spoke in a deep voice and when her eyes met his she blushed.

She knew what he wanted and it was something she wanted for herself, but the barrier of having no money kept them invisibly but completely apart.

When dinner was finished, the ladies left the room but not for long.

The Prince's favourite games were waiting for him and card tables were set out in the drawing room.

As Galina had heard, he often played for what some would find high stakes, but not quite so overwhelming as in other fashionable house parties.

The Prince was voted forty thousand pounds a year by Parliament and received substantial revenues from the Duchy of Cornwall.

But he had come to learn that he must be modest in his gambling if he was to enjoy his other expensive tastes.

Galina recognised that Lord Bramton would find it impossible even to lose a few pounds at the card table.

It was because the Princess herself was so sensible and intelligent that she was aware that some people would have this difficulty.

She therefore insisted that her guests, however old and distinguished should play nursery favourites with her – such as general post, blindman's buff or hunt the slipper.

Galina was surprised, but she joined in and enjoyed every moment of all the games.

Several of the gentlemen including Lord Bramton joined the ladies and they were all soon laughing helplessly at the antics of the competitors.

It was nearly midnight when the Princess said that it was now time to retire and most of the ladies, especially the older ones, were only too eager to comply.

They walked upstairs without saying goodnight or interrupting their host at his card table.

Lord Bramton too like some of the older gentlemen was delighted to retire.

It was well known that the Prince of Wales was always prepared to settle down and gamble the night away and it was incorrect for the gentlemen playing with him to retire to bed before he did.

Upstairs Galina said goodnight to Ellie-May.

She felt it had been an exciting and unusual evening and she admitted to herself that what she had enjoyed more than anything was that Lord Bramton had been at her side.

She had noticed too that Sir Christopher was one of the young gentlemen present who kept Ellie-May amused.

She had not had any chance to speak to Mr. Farlow, but she was quite certain that it had been the most thrilling evening he had ever spent.

She suspected that he would settle himself down to enjoy the gambling and it would not worry him if it went on until dawn.

Before she retired Sir Christopher had whispered to Galina,

"Ladies are not expected to appear before luncheon. You spend the morning as you please – reading, gossiping or exploring the garden."

"That is what I will do," Galina said later to Lord Bramton. "I want to look at the daffodils."

"So do I," he replied.

When they said goodnight, he murmured so that no one else could hear,

"I will be waiting for you at eleven o'clock."

*

Galina had breakfast in her bedroom and Ellie-May joined her.

"Are you enjoying yourself?" enquired Galina.

Ellie-May clasped her hands together.

"It's all wonderful and I know that Papa will want to give you a marvellous present for arranging this for us. So you must think of what you particularly want."

Galina felt like saying that a few thousand dollars would be better than anything else, but instead she said,

"Your father has been very helpful to us by renting Ranmore House in London and if anything my brother and I ought to give *him* a present."

Ellie-May laughed.

"Now don't be silly. Papa likes giving presents and the more they cost, the more you know he can afford it!"

"Then it should be quite easy to think of something, but it would be more exciting if it was a surprise."

The two girls chatted away until it was ten o'clock and then they dressed.

Ellie-May was ready first and said that she would go downstairs and see what the other ladies were doing.

"I will not be long after you," promised Galina.

Then as she looked out of the window she saw Lord Bramton. He was walking away from the house towards the daffodils under the trees.

She wanted to be with him.

Nothing else mattered to her not even Sandringham or the Prince of Wales.

She ran down the stairs.

She could hear women's voices chatting in one of the reception rooms and yet no one noticed her, except the footmen on duty, as she slipped out of the front door and across the lawn.

Lord Bramton was gazing at the daffodils and did not see her until she reached his side.

"Good morning," she smiled up at him.

"Let's go down to the lake, Galina, so that we can talk without being interrupted."

They moved away through the trees.

Galina felt that the daffodils all around them made it seem unreal, almost as if she was walking in a dream.

When they reached the lake there was one wooden seat at the edge of the water.

They sat down and Lord Bramton asked her,

"Are you enjoying yourself?"

"It is all so thrilling, but I am so glad you are here too, otherwise I might annoy His Royal Highness."

"I just don't think he could be annoyed with you for very long. You are far too lovely. I found it difficult to go to sleep last night because you looked so beautiful in that new gown."

"I have to thank Mr. Farlow for it. He insisted that Ellie-May and I were dressed for the part."

"I have never seen a man so happy. He told me at breakfast that this would put up his standing in New York, which is already very high, by leaps and bounds."

"He is lucky that His Royal Highness was curious about him and Ellie-May – or we would not be here."

"But we are here and I am more grateful than I can possibly say that I am here with you, Galina."

Then as if he was forcing himself, he looked away from her at the silver water in front of them.

"It's no use. I try to be sensible, but I find it almost impossible to think of anything but you, you and *you*!"

Galina drew in her breath.

"And I think of you too," she said in a small voice.

There was silence for a moment and then he added,

"It is no use fighting against love, it is stronger than both of us. Shall we be married? I expect that I could find work of some sort if I closed up the house."

"But you cannot do that!" exclaimed Galina. "And I have to think of Georgie and help him if I can."

Lord Bramton sighed.

"I know that I am talking nonsense, Galina, but it is hard to think sensibly when I want you so much and God knows I need you."

Galina slipped her hand into his.

"We have to be brave for the moment and see what happens. Perhaps Georgie will come back from America having found an oil well."

"If he does, then I will go out and see if I can find one too. But it would be a mistake to be too optimistic."

Galina knew that he was thinking of her rather than himself.

"I just feel in my bones that something will happen to help us, so we just have to be brave until it does."

Lord Bramton smiled at her and sighed,

"I love you so much, Galina. No one else could be so sensible and at the same time so utterly adorable."

His fingers tightened on her hand until it hurt.

"We have to believe that our prayers are heard and that things will not be quite as bad as we anticipate. As you say, Georgie may easily find an oil well or perhaps he will find an American millionairess in New York."

"That is where they are, but equally, I do think he would be much happier with an English girl."

"I know how unhappy I would be without you."

"We must not stay here too long, Victor. I joined you as I could see you from the window, but perhaps the Princess would be shocked at my not being chaperoned."

"I think myself that she would understand a little of what we are feeling, but you are quite right, my darling, we will go back and make ourselves pleasant."

Galina looked around at the lake and the daffodils.

"This is a fairyland and all we need is a magician's wand to bring us what we both need and that is money.

"Not for ourselves, but for our houses that are both a part of England. That is why we have to fight for them even though it is now so difficult for us and then we can be together as we wish to be."

"I know what you are saying, my dearest, and it is just what you would say. I want you so desperately that it is such agony to think that you may never be mine."

Galina gave a little cry.

"That is what you must *not* think. You must believe that we will be together and that it *will* be possible for us."

Lord Bramton did not reply and she carried on,

"I know now I love you and I will never be happy with anyone else, but I also believe that in some wonderful magical way it will be possible for us to love each other."

Lord Bramton raised her hand to his lips and softly and gently he kissed each of her fingers.

Then he kissed the centre of her palm.

"You are quite right, my precious, we will not give up hope. It is hard, so very hard at the moment, to face a future which will be unbelievably empty without you."

As he finished speaking, he rose to his feet and she knew he was making himself do as she had suggested and take her back to the house.

They walked back in silence.

Only when the front door was just in front of them did they look at each other.

There was no need for words.

The expression in Lord Bramton's eyes told Galina how much he loved her.

She could not prevent a sob coming from her lips as she walked up the steps.

*

In the afternoon they all attended the Flower Show, which the Princess was to open in the Village Hall.

The house party went first and was received by the Lord Lieutenant and the Vicar.

At exactly two o'clock the Princess arrived and was escorted onto the platform.

She was looking particularly stunning in a gown of her favourite blue and she wore a very pretty hat decorated with flowers to match it.

She spoke clearly and charmingly as she opened the Flower Show and her speech was greeted with a loud burst of applause from the crowd.

People clapped and continued to clap until the Lord Lieutenant raised his hands for silence.

He thanked Her Royal Highness for coming and he said he was certain that the Flower Show would produce a great deal of money for the Cottage Hospital.

He requested those present to put what they could afford into a box at the door as they left the room.

He then thanked everyone for their support for the hospital which served the whole neighbourhood.

Galina glanced in the direction of Mr. Farlow as the Lord Lieutenant finished speaking.

She was not surprised to see him writing a cheque and she thought it was intelligent of him to realise that he would be asked for money during the afternoon.

The Princess moved slowly from the Hall shaking hands with a number of people as she did so and then went into the rooms where the flowers were on display.

Mr. Farlow then walked up to the Lord Lieutenant and Galina heard him introduce himself. He gave him the cheque and the Lord Lieutenant thanked him.

And then as he glanced at the cheque, he was most profuse in his gratitude.

Galina was amused.

She thought that when Mr. Farlow first spoke to the Lord Lieutenant that he had been polite and yet he was not particularly effusive at being spoken to by a man to whom he had not been introduced.

However, he must have appreciated, when he saw the cheque, who Mr. Farlow was.

A few seconds later she saw him whispering to Her Royal Highness.

It was not until they had returned to the house and were having tea in the drawing room that the Princess said to Mr. Farlow,

"Thank you so very much for your most kind and generous donation to our hospital. I am so touched by it."

"I thought your appeal, Your Royal Highness, was very moving," he answered.

"Our hospital does a lot of good and what you have given us will make it easier for us, in the coming year, to provide more beds and therefore more patients than we can accommodate at the moment."

She was obviously extremely grateful.

Galina felt at least someone had benefitted from the party at Sandringham.

*

The evening passed in very much the same way as the evening before.

As everyone knew each other better, there seemed to be more laughter and there was definitely a more relaxed atmosphere than there had been the previous night.

It was when they were going to bed that the Prince announced unexpectedly,

"As tomorrow is Sunday, and we are all going to Church in the morning, I have decided in the afternoon that I would like to visit the famous house of one of our guests. Bramton Priory is, I am told, one of the most ancient and significant houses in England."

He glanced towards Lord Bramton as he spoke and asked him,

"Is that true?"

"So I have always been told, Your Royal Highness, and it will be a great pleasure for me to show you some of the treasures collected by my ancestors over the years."

"That is what we are looking forward to," said the Prince. "We will leave after luncheon and I understand it will not take more than an hour to reach Bramton Priory."

"It is a great honour and it will be my pleasure to show you around my home."

Their Royal Highnesses now retired and Ellie-May started talking about the Flower Show.

"I am going to stage my own Flower Show in New York, she announced, "and I am certain that everyone will think it interesting especially the original arrangements."

Galina thought that Flower Shows were something that only occurred in the country and not in Cities, but she did not want to dampen Ellie-May's enthusiasm.

She kissed her good night saying,

"We will discuss it in the morning. And I am sure

you will have more to talk about when you have seen Lord Bramton's house."

"I have not seen half of this house yet," Ellie-May protested.

"It is very impressive, but I promise you that Lord Bramton's will be more exciting."

When Galina climbed into her bed, she prayed very hard for a long time.

Maybe something would happen that would enable Lord Bramton to keep his house open and he could afford to live there.

Yet the only practical solution she could think of at that moment and which tortured her to her soul was that he should marry Ellie-May.

There would be no more problems for him, except those that would affect his heart, and it would please Mr. Farlow that they were so close to Sandringham.

Galina knew if he did marry anyone else, it would be impossible for her ever to love anyone in the same way as she loved him now.

'*I love him*. I do love him,' she whispered into her pillow. 'Oh, please, please God, make it possible for us to be together. Even if we are poor and have to live in a cave, we would still have each other.'

Then because the idea of losing him was so painful, she felt tears running down her cheeks.

*

The next morning as soon as they had had breakfast it was time to go to Church.

There was a special pew for the Prince and Princess of Wales and several others for Royal guests.

The Church was naturally decorated with daffodils and the choir sang extremely well for a village.

The Vicar preached for a little over ten minutes and Galina was certain that he was restricted into giving a short sermon by His Royal Highness.

It was a relief to be driving back to the house well before luncheon.

Galina felt very excited when just after two o'clock they climbed into the Royal carriages again and set off for Bramton Priory.

Travelling with her was Lord Bramton, Ellie-May and Sir Christopher – the two men sitting opposite the two girls.

Sir Christopher remarked,

"I have been looking for descriptions of your house, Victor, in some of His Royal Highness's books, but so far I have not found an answer to everything I want to know, so I hope you intend to be our guide and informant."

Lord Bramton smiled.

"As the house has been closed up, I shall have to do all you suggest and much more."

"But surely," Ellie-May asked, "you have someone to look after your treasures when you are not there."

"There is a very old couple who have been with my father for very many years and who have nowhere else to go. They are in charge. I am also very fortunate that so far I have not been burgled."

Galina gave a little cry.

"That would be a horrible disaster."

"I know, but it is always dangerous to leave a house of that size without plenty of servants to take care of it."

He spoke somewhat bitterly and Galina thought it a mistake to pursue the subject further.

Then Ellie-May piped up,

"One old lady last night said she had seen a little of your house because she had bribed the housekeeper!"

Lord Bramton stared at her.

"Who said that?" he asked in a surprised voice.

"The Countess of Overton, yes, that was her name. She said that what she saw was so unique she thought that it ought to be in a museum."

"And you say that she bribed the housekeeper, who I suppose must have been my caretaker, to take her round."

"Yes and there was another lady – I don't know her name – who laughed and declared she had done the same at Marlborough House when the family were away."

"I can easily understand," came in Sir Christopher, "visitors from overseas being clever enough to find a way to see round these houses. We have a number of people coming to Sandringham when His Royal Highness is not there who beg the servants on their knees to be allowed to look inside, but I believe they always refuse."

"That is what I believed too," said Lord Bramton.

He did not say anything more, but he was thinking, however, that he could well understand his caretakers, who he could only pay a pittance, being very grateful to receive something however small from passing visitors.

Galina was well aware of what he was thinking and it suddenly occurred to her that he could open his house to the public.

If they paid a fairly substantial sum for the privilege it would at least make it possible for him to keep the house in good order and he could pay servants to look after it.

'I must talk to Victor about my idea,' she thought.

She wondered as they drove on if he would think it a good one, but she had the uneasy feeling that he might think it sacrilege to his ancestors and the collection itself.

'I cannot think why, because it is something to be proud of and there is no doubt that all visitors to England expect to find ancient monuments to interest them. Just as if one goes to America, like Georgie, one expects to find new ideas and inventions.'

They drove on and then turned eventually through some gates which looked rather dilapidated. The lodges on each side were empty and in a very bad repair.

The drive was lined with ancient oaks which were beautiful, but they had not been attended to and branches had fallen to the ground.

As she saw the house ahead, Galina gave a gasp.

It was beautiful in the sunshine, a perfect example of mediaeval architecture.

She could well understand why Lord Bramton was so proud of his ancestral home.

There was a large lake in front of the house and an old bridge over it which needed repair.

As they drove nearer to the house, Galina could see that a number of windows were cracked or broken.

The courtyard had not been brushed and it needed fresh gravel. There were weeds growing in the steps that led up to the front door.

The carriages drew up and Lord Bramton opened the front door which on his instructions had been unlocked.

"I am afraid, Your Royal Highnesses," he said to the Prince and Princess, "you will find things are dusty as I have not been able to afford any servants for a long time."

Dusty or not it was a vast hall that they walked into where the ancient monks had received travellers or anyone who sought their help and blessing.

There were priceless pictures on the walls which immediately commanded the Prince of Wales's attention.

Then Lord Bramton led the party through several rooms where there were many collections of pictures and furniture.

Every chair and every table was valuable.

In one room there was a large collection of Dresden china that made the Princess exclaim with excitement. She was equally enthralled by another room which contained a huge collection of ivory.

Among this was a carving of a Sumo wrestler and a carved ivory okimono of a farmer with a bamboo pole and an old carving of a Chinese scholar and a monkey with a toad on his back!

Then Lord Bramton took them to his collection of jade and these as well were fantastic. Their colour and the exquisite carving was, Galina considered, something that anyone would be exceedingly proud of.

She was thrilled with a striding dragon, whilst the Princess said what she liked more than anything else was a green jade rectangular box with dragon-head handles.

"It goes all the way back the Qing Dynasty," Lord Bramton said, "and is, I believe, extremely ancient."

They viewed other rooms and next Lord Bramton guided them into a room that Galina knew he was longing to show her.

It contained his collection of statues that had been brought by his great-great-grandfather from Greece.

As soon as she glanced at them, she realised why, although it seemed conceited, he compared her to them.

Some of the Goddesses, although they had lost their arms, were undoubtedly exquisitely lovely. There were no sculptures in the world as beautiful and artistic as those the Greeks had produced thousands of years ago.

The Prince and Princess were enchanted by them.

"Oh, look at this one, Edward!" the Princess kept exclaiming. "Have you ever seen anything so wonderful? And this! And this!"

She ran from one statue to another.

Finally when they had just about exhausted all their exclamations of delight at the Greek statues, Lord Bramton took them all into the Chapel, which did not appear to have suffered so much from neglect.

A gold and bejewelled cross on the altar with six gold candlesticks beside it was a very fine piece of work.

The altar itself was of carved marble and sculptured by a master hand and was more magnificent than anything Galina had seen in any Church.

Some stained glass windows had been broken, but the sunshine coming through those intact seemed to cast a magic light over the Chapel.

It was different to anything Galina had ever seen.

'It is beautiful, it is Holy and it is blessed by God,' she sighed to herself.

Even as the words came to her, she glanced at Lord Bramton and she realised that he was thinking the same.

She knew, too, that he wanted to kneel in front of the altar beside her while a Priest blessed their marriage.

Because the Chapel had such a spiritual atmosphere everyone seemed to sense that the tour was over.

They returned to a huge reception room almost in silence and then the Prince and Princess walked to their carriage and the party followed them.

Only as Galina brought up the rear, was she aware that Mr. Farlow was not with them.

Lord Bramton came to her side.

"Now you have seen my home, Galina!"

"It is beautiful, Victor, so beautiful that I know now that you must save it and somehow we have to find a way."

She thought again that he should open the house to the public, but this was not the moment to air the subject.

Ellie-May joined them.

"Where is Papa?" she asked.

"I will go and find him," suggested Lord Bramton.

He was just about to do so, when Mr. Farlow came hurrying down the passage.

"I'm sorry if I've kept you waiting," he said. "I just had to have another look at your ivory collection and also at the pictures we passed by too quickly."

"There is a great deal more that I could show you," Lord Bramton proposed. "But I did not want to bore Their Royal Highnessses."

"Well, I want to see everything you possess," Mr. Farlow insisted. "It's wonderful, amazing and different to anything I've ever seen in any other country."

"I rather pride myself that the Priory is unique."

"I'm not surprised."

Then, as he realised the carriages were waiting for him, he hurried down the steps.

Ellie-May and Galina climbed in and Lord Bramton and Sir Christopher followed them.

"I just think you are the luckiest man in the world," Ellie-May asserted enthusiastically. "I just can't imagine anyone having such a fine collection."

"There is just one item I would wish to add to it," Lord Bramton answered her.

He looked at Galina as he spoke.

CHAPTER SIX

Georgie came down for breakfast and two servants started to serve him.

He thought now as he had when he went to bed last night how lucky he was not to be in some cheap lodging house.

Instead of which he was now staying in one of the largest and most comfortable houses in Fifth Avenue.

Mr. Wilbur entered and Georgie started to rise.

"Don't get up, my dear boy," he declared. "I'm not used to such good manners in New York."

"I was enjoying breakfast and thinking how grateful I am to you for having me here."

"I like having you."

"Are we to travel to Pennsylvania today?"

Georgie could not help feeling that it was a mistake to waste too much time before he started on the real object of his journey.

Mr. Wilbur sat down at the table and the servants brought him a dish of eggs and bacon.

When they had left the room he turned to Georgie,

"I have arranged for us to leave for Pennsylvania tonight and I think you will be interested in seeing the new sleeping cars on our train."

"I am sure you are more advanced than we are."

Mr. Wilbur did not answer – he was obviously deep in thought and then he remarked,

"I've been thinking since we met how much I've enjoyed your company and how interesting it is for me to be able to show you around."

"I should be thanking you. As you rightly pointed out yourself I am a complete greenhorn and I am sure that I should get into trouble if you were not there to guide me."

"It's not just guiding, but of having the company of a young man, who I think has a very good brain."

Georgie laughed.

"Now you are paying me a nice compliment I really appreciate and I will certainly report it to my sister when I return home."

"You have not talked much about your own home," Mr. Wilbur commented. "In fact, I have a feeling that I've done all the talking."

"I am so very intent on learning from you and being inspired by the brilliant way you have been so successful."

"And you yourself want to be successful?"

"It is something I have to be," answered Georgie, "and a great deal depends on it."

There was silence for a moment as Georgie helped himself to some toast and marmalade.

"What I have been thinking," Mr. Wilbur continued slowly, "is that, as you so wish to explore the oil fields, we might go into partnership together – "

For a moment Georgie did not think he had heard correctly. He put down the spoonful of marmalade he was conveying to his plate and stared at Mr. Wilbur.

"Did you say – *partnership*?"

"You made me recognise as we were coming across the Atlantic how much I have missed in life by not having a son. I have very few relatives and I have often wondered what will happen to my possessions when I die."

"You might get married," suggested Georgie.

"I've thought about it, of course I have, but I have never met any woman who did not bore me after a short time and who I am quite certain would love me for myself and not for my money."

"I am sorry – "

"You needn't be. I've been perfectly happy on my own. But now I've met you, I would like to help you make the fortune you say you need. We have a great number of interests in common in the development of new ideas."

Georgie drew in his breath and then he asked in a rather small voice,

"Are you really saying I can be your partner?"

"That is exactly what I want and we will go to the Solicitors this morning and draw up a proper partnership agreement between us. Everything I invest in from now on will be shared with *you*."

"But I have no money to invest."

Mr. Wilbur smiled.

"I'm aware of that, my boy, but that is immaterial. I've quite enough for both of us until the dollars flow in, as I expect them to do."

There was silence because Georgie was completely overcome by the idea.

Then he exclaimed,

"I cannot believe this is really happening to me."

Mr. Wilbur laughed loudly.

"I know that feeling, but I also know we'll have a very happy and interesting partnership together."

Again there was silence and then Georgie broke it rather tentatively,

"I think before we go any further I must tell you the truth."

He realised Mr. Wilbur stiffened before he asked,

"*The truth*! What do you mean by the truth?"

"I have been travelling under an assumed name and actually I am the seventh Earl of Ranmore."

It was Mr. Wilbur's turn to look surprised.

"*The Earl of Ranmore*! Well, so why in Heaven's name then are you now calling yourself Mr. Donaldson?"

"It's the name on the passport of a friend of mine who was killed in an accident and I thought too, as you do not have many titles in America, it would create too much interest for a man who had come out to make his fortune and is, at this present moment, almost penniless."

"But how can you be if you're an Earl?"

"Very easily as it happens. I would not have been able to afford this trip if one of your countrymen had not rented my large house in London and paid a great deal for doing so."

"Who is that?"

Mr. Wilbur looked curiously at him.

"Mr. Craig Farlow. Perhaps you know him?"

"Of course, I know him. A jolly good fellow and he's been a friend of mine for years. I knew he was going to England to find a titled husband for his daughter. Why don't you marry her?"

Georgie smiled.

"I did think of it, but quite frankly as a man I like to have money of my own, and if I do marry I want to be in love with my wife."

"Quite right!" Mr. Wilbur said loudly. "Absolutely right, but now tell me about yourself and the house Farlow is staying in."

"Actually I have two houses. One in London which

I think you would call enormous and a house in the country which is hundreds of years old and has a finer collection of pictures than any other house in England."

Mr. Wilbur stared at him in astonishment.

"And you say you have *no* money?"

"It does sound ridiculous, but I literally do not have a penny to bless myself with and a large number of debts."

"How? I just don't understand."

Georgie explained how the houses and possessions of the aristocracy in England were entailed from one heir to another.

"It is the reason why the great houses have all been preserved over the centuries and I can honestly tell you that my country house is an antique masterpiece standing in a thousand acres, but I cannot afford to live in it."

"So that is why you have come to America?"

"Exactly! Because things cannot go on as they are. I have been thanking God every day we have been at sea, because you were telling me all I wanted to know about the American oil wells."

"Well, tomorrow you'll see them for yourself. Now breakfast is finished, we'll go to my Solicitor and draw up a partnership agreement between us."

"Are you quite certain that you want me?"

"That's a stupid question," Mr. Wilbur replied. "If I wanted you as Johnson Donaldson, you'll be far more use to me as the Earl of Ranmore and instantly I shall be one up on Craig Farlow!"

Georgie laughed.

He had heard how the millionaires on Fifth Avenue vied with each other for prestige as well as riches.

They set off in Mr. Wilbur's smart carriage and he

was asking Georgie question after question about the life he lived in London.

He enquired whether he knew the Prince of Wales and if he had ever been to Windsor Castle.

When Georgie said "yes" to the last two questions, Mr. Wilbur sat back with an air of satisfaction.

"Now there's no need for me to be envious of the Vanderbilts, the Rockerfellers or Farlow for that matter! With you as a partner, I'll have them grinding their teeth!"

"I shouldn't be too sure. There are, I believe, quite a number of rich American heiresses coming to London in search of a title. I am told you already have quite a number of Italian Princes on Fifth Avenue."

Mr. Wilbur nodded.

"That's true, but in my opinion an English Lord or rather an Earl is worth half a dozen of them!"

"I hope you go on thinking that."

They went into the Solicitors office.

Georgie remained silent while Mr. Wilbur set down exactly what he wanted in their partnership agreement.

As far as he could make out the details, it would be of enormous benefit to him and he hoped that Mr. Wilbur's share would be satisfying for him.

While still at the Solicitors, Mr. Wilbur said he had already put quite a lot of money into the development of the telephone.

However, he would like to add much more and he was also going to finance a new idea he had only heard of just as he was leaving for England.

"What can that be," asked the Solicitor.

"It's called a typewriter. I believe it was invented some years ago, but it is only now arousing interest. From what I've heard and seen it should make a fortune once it catches on."

The Solicitor smiled.

"I hope you are right, sir, as you usually are. And, of course, the next thing I feel you will be interested in is what they call the 'heavier than air flying machine'."

"I've heard about it too, but I don't think that you'll find that on the market for some time."

Georgie was listening entranced.

Then he signed his name to the document to which Mr. Wilbur had already put his.

As he did so he saw the look of satisfaction in the older man's face and he knew he was doing him a favour that he had not expected.

After an excellent luncheon they left New York in a highly comfortable train.

While they were travelling, Georgie persuaded Mr. Wilbur to talk again about the oil towns.

He made it sound fantastic with his descriptions of rowdy saloons, gambling for high stakes and life and death duels.

When they had first started drilling one or two men were killed every day, but it had settled down now.

But it could still be very dangerous for a greenhorn.

"I really cannot tell you," enthused Georgie, "how incredibly grateful I am to you for your protection."

"You'll be protected all right," Mr. Wilbur assured him, "and my men will be guarding us all the time."

"Are they working on any particular oil well at the moment?" enquired Georgie.

"We closed one just before I came to England as it was empty. But I understand they've heard of another and are awaiting my instructions."

Georgie wondered if he should say that Mr. Farlow had heard of one too in the same area.

He still had the telegram Galina had sent him in his pocket, but he thought he would leave things as they were.

After all he had been so lucky to become a partner of Mr. Wilbur's and there was therefore no reason now for him to involve Mr. Farlow in any way.

Especially as, at the back of his mind, he thought it was cheating.

'I have been blessed,' he thought, 'in a way I never expected. And from now on I am going to play it straight as I always have in my life.'

With a new sense of relief he had not felt for years, Georgie slept peacefully on the train.

They arrived the next morning and drove from the train to the oil fields and this gave Georgie a chance to see a little of the country.

The first thing he noticed were the wild flowers that he knew would delight Galina.

There were hepatica, wild honeysuckle, dog's tooth violets, as the American's called them, and anemones.

What interested him more than anything else was the animal and bird life and Mr. Wilbur had already told him there were still primeval forests in Pennsylvania.

"There are still black bears, although not so many of them. And panthers, wild-cats, wolves and elks."

"They really do interest me. I would love to see the black bears."

Mr. Wilbur smiled.

"You are more likely to see white-tailed deer and smaller animals such as racoons, skunks and woodchucks which are common around here."

"And what about the birds?" Georgie asked him.

"Oh, you'll see them right enough. Ruffed grouse, quail and pheasants if the oilmen haven't eaten them all!"

Georgie hoped he would have the chance of going into the forest and he would love to see the rivers that he had read about in a book he had found in the library of the ship when they were crossing the Atlantic.

'The truth is,' he told himself, 'I should have taken a great deal more time going through my own library. I am sure that there are books on America which will tell me far more than I know at the moment.'

But it was too late now and he knew that what he had really come for was just ahead of him.

Mr. Wilbur had not exaggerated the excitement and fantastic appearance of the oil fields.

They arrived and were taken to what he understood was the most comfortable inn in town, although it looked shabby and rough after the comfort of Fifth Avenue.

What he was really excited about were the oil wells themselves and these were to be seen everywhere.

As Mr. Wilbur explained to him it was 'every man for himself', a well-established American tradition.

There was no one around who was not desperately trying to discover a new source.

It was, as Mr. Wilbur put it,

"Just like putting your right hand into a sack and not knowing what you're going to pull out. It might be a seam of coal, a vein of silver or what is more desirable than anything else, a gusher of oil!"

Then Georgie learnt they would work the well to extinction, ravish the land and then move on.

What he found extraordinary was that many of the

'oil towns' as they were called had produced their 'fill' and had then gone back to grass and were forgotten.

"What we really require is efficient organisation," Mr. Wilbur remarked as he showed Georgie round. "At the moment everyone's scrambling for anything they can grab and that means waste as well as unnecessary antagonism which we can well do without."

Georgie knew exactly what he was saying.

The second day they were there, the oil men in Mr. Wilbur's pay drilled down to where they had told him they suspected oil was to be found.

They were *right*.

The excitement was overwhelming.

However they were aware that evening when they went back to their hotel there were many black looks.

There were also murmurs of 'some people are too damned lucky!'

*

They stayed for five days seeing the oil surging up from the well.

"There's more oil here," Mr. Wilbur emphasised, "but I'm determined to look elsewhere and I've got my eye on gold."

"Gold!" exclaimed Georgie.

It was not what he had expected.

"Gold was found twelve years ago in Colorado and I'm convinced it can be found in Nevada and other places. Again it is just a question of organisation and good luck."

"And you have both."

"So have *you* now," Mr. Wilbur reminded him.

The oil well looked like being one of the best in the Pennsylvania oil field of Titusville.

The two of them went back to New York delighted with themselves.

"Now, I shall have to return home," said Georgie. "But I am hoping that you will come over next month, so that I can show you my house and you will meet my sister. Then I thought we might both come back again before the end of the summer."

"But, of course, my dear boy. I will miss you and you must remember as partners that we have a great many more explorations to make."

"That will be just superb. I still cannot believe that I am not dreaming and that all that black muck oozing out of the ground will really turn into dollars and pounds!"

Mr. Wilbur chuckled.

"You'll soon learn to take it as a matter of course."

He was, as Georgie knew, absolutely delighted that their first oil well of their partnership had proved to have a great future.

"The deeper it is the more valuable, and from what my men have already discovered, it looks as if it will feed us for at least a couple of years."

It was difficult for Georgie to appreciate how much this meant.

He only knew that he was the luckiest man alive.

He had not telegraphed Galina with the good news for the simple reason that he was afraid like fairy gold, it might disappear over night!

And then everyone would be disappointed.

'I will tell her all about it when I reach home,' he decided.

He was anxious now that everything had turned out so brilliantly to return to England as soon as possible.

However, he had to stay a little longer in New York just to make Mr. Wilbur happy – he was just so excited at having a titled partner he was growing very fond of.

Georgie therefore felt he must do what he wanted and stay a few days longer.

The day after they returned to New York, they were walking slowly down Fifth Avenue to attend an invitation to luncheon with one of Mr. Wilbur's friends.

Suddenly a very pretty girl stepped out of a carriage and cried,

"Georgie! It cannot be you!"

Georgie turned round.

He saw someone running towards him and he held out his arms.

"Monica!" he exclaimed.

"What can you be doing in New York?" she asked excitedly.

Nearly three years ago he had been very attracted to Monica, the daughter of a distinguished diplomat.

They had spent a great deal of time together one summer – and he had fallen in love with her.

But he was already well aware that things were so bad financially that it would be quite impossible for him to marry anyone.

He kissed Monica after a party where they had sat together at dinner and danced nearly every dance with her.

He had, when he went home, turned over and over in his mind whether he would ask her to share his poverty with him.

Then he knew it would not work.

No woman would ever want to live in an enormous house in the country with no servants.

When he returned to London, Monica had left and he learned later that her father, Sir Desmond Wilcourt, had been sent as British Consul to New York.

He longed to write to her, but thought it a mistake.

He knew now, as he took her hand in his, she was even lovelier than she had been when he last saw her.

"I cannot believe it is you, Monica. I've wondered if I would ever see you again. Are you coming back to England?"

Monica nodded.

"Papa has finished his time here and we hope that he may be offered a senior position at the Foreign Office in London."

Then Georgie realised that Mr. Wilbur was beside them.

"Forgive me," he apologised, "for not introducing you to my host, Mr. Clint Wilbur."

Monica held out her hand.

"I have indeed heard of you, Mr. Wilbur, and the success you have had in discovering oil in Pennsylvania."

"I've been extremely lucky," he replied, "but now I have a partner I will be luckier still!"

Monica did not understand and Georgie explained,

"You have to congratulate me, Monica. Mr. Wilbur has been kind enough to make me his partner and it is the most fantastic thing that has ever happened to me."

"But of course it is, and I know that Papa will want to hear all about it. So both of you, please come to dinner tonight. I know we are at home for once."

Georgie looked at Mr. Wilbur.

"We are delighted to accept," he answered and they arranged a time.

Then Monica waved at them and disappeared into a shop, while they walked on to their luncheon appointment.

"She's a very pretty girl," commented Mr. Wilbur.

"I have always thought so, but she has become even prettier since she has been in America."

That evening they dined at the Consulate with Sir Desmond. There were two other diplomats present, one of whom had a rather attractive wife.

It was a party Mr. Wilbur enjoyed whilst Georgie was very conscious of Monica.

After dinner the men played bridge as Monica took Georgie on a tour of the Consulate.

It was an interesting building and flew a vast Union Jack to impress the Americans.

Monica took Georgie into the conservatory to show him the orchids her father was cultivating.

He closed the door behind them.

"I have missed you, Monica, more than I can tell you, since you left England."

"And I have missed *you*," she whispered.

They looked at each other and then Georgie said,

"You know I had nothing to offer you at the time."

She nodded.

"I did realise that, but I cried into my pillow every night while I was crossing the Atlantic."

Georgie pulled her into his arms.

"I love you, Monica. I have always loved you and now everything is very different. So different I can hardly appreciate it myself."

"You mean because that rich Mr. Wilbur has made you his partner? I think he is a very nice man."

"He is wonderful, marvellous and the kindest man on earth, especially as now I can do what I want to do."

He pulled Monica even closer to him and then he was kissing her.

Kissing her wildly, demandingly, passionately, as if, having lost her, he was determined never to lose her again.

"I love you, Georgie," murmured Monica. "I love you and there has never been anyone else."

"And I have never loved anyone but you. We will be married as soon as you return to England."

She looked up at him and the radiant expression on her face told him without words what she was feeling.

Then he was kissing her again – kissing her until they were both breathless.

The conservatory was a Paradise because they had found each other again and there would be no more parting in the future.

The following day Georgie sent a large bouquet of orchids to Monica – he had to borrow the money from Mr. Wilbur to buy them.

When he had told him he was penniless Mr. Wilbur had laughed.

"More foolish of you for not telling me earlier! But I presume you'd have spent most of your money crossing the Atlantic in comfort."

"I should have travelled Third Class," he admitted, "but some instinct or my Guardian Angel told me that you would be aboard and that is how it all started."

Mr. Wilbur chuckled.

"It started for me too. Now what I am going to do is to pay a decent amount into your bank in London from my bank here. We will settle it up when the dollars start flowing in from our oil well and our other investments."

Georgie could only thank him.

When he learnt how much Mr. Wilbur had paid into his bank account, he found it difficult to believe it was true.

He was sensible enough to realise that Mr. Wilbur possessed a very shrewd brain and there was no doubt that the many different projects in which they were investing as partners would turn out to be successes.

He was quite certain too, when he saw it, that even the typewriter would eventually 'catch on', as Mr. Wilbur put it so succinctly, in every office and shop.

As to the telephone, Mr. Wilbur made Georgie use the one he possessed and again he thought it was the most enthralling thing he had ever done.

He talked to one of Mr. Wilbur's friends and learnt that Mr. Wilbur was having a telephone installed in his oil field, so that he would be able to talk daily to the men who were working there.

'There are endless possibilities for the telephone,' Georgie thought.

He told himself once again how lucky he was.

When finally the time arrived for him to return to London, Mr. Wilbur had already booked for him the most comfortable First Class cabin aboard the Steamship he was to travel in.

He was bowed aboard almost as if he was Royalty.

He felt as he observed the respect with which Mr. Wilbur was treated by everyone in New York that he was really the Royalty of America because he was so rich.

'Men like him have the world at their feet,' Georgie thought. 'And please God there is now a big chance I will be one of them.'

Before he left he visited a jeweller's shop with Mr. Wilbur and bought a very attractive bracelet for Galina.

"She has been wonderful to me while we have been struggling so hard to keep our heads above water," Georgie told Mr. Wilbur.

"You take your sister that," he said, "and I'll take the necklace to match it when I come over."

"You are spoiling us." Georgie protested.

Mr. Wilbur put his hand on his shoulder.

"I've no wife, no children and very few relatives, so I've got to spoil someone and that, my dear boy, is *you*."

As the Steamship sailed out of New York harbour, Georgie waved goodbye.

He thought Mr. Wilbur looked somehow pathetic standing alone on the quay.

'I will make it up to him some way or another,' he vowed to himself.

He knew that like Mr. Farlow he would be thrilled and delighted with his house in Park Lane and when he had made his country house more habitable with the proceeds from his new well, Mr. Wilbur would enjoy it too.

When he retired that night, he thought that when he had his own children, and that was just what he did want, Mr. Wilbur would almost feel as if they were his own.

Of course he would be asked to be the Godfather of each one of them.

'The way I can really pay him back,' he murmured to himself, 'is by giving him the love and affection he has always missed because he has been on his own.'

Then his thoughts turned to Galina and how brave and supporting she had always been to him.

'It is love that we all pray for, and however much money one has, it is not the same as having those you love put their arms around you.'

The Steamship was one of the fastest and he was fortunate that the sea was calm.

Because he was travelling under his own name, he was seated at the Captain's table for every meal and was treated respectfully by everyone aboard.

They were, however, not a particularly interesting collection and so Georgie spent most of his time reading in the library.

Fortunately the books were mostly about America.

'It is now my country as I own so much in it,' he reflected, 'so I must learn all about it. I cannot expect Mr. Wilbur to tell me everything I need to know.'

He had sent a telegram to Galina to tell her when he was arriving and telling her that he would go straight from Liverpool to London by train.

He thought with satisfaction how thrilling it would be when she learnt that he had been successful in America.

Now at last they could get down to saving Ranmore Park and make it as habitable as in his grandfather's time.

Then he pondered about Monica and how happy he would be there with her.

At the same time he was a little apprehensive just in case she and Galina did not get on together.

He had never mentioned Monica to his sister.

As there was no chance of being able to marry her, he had been trying not to think about her or how much she meant to him.

Now he could recall all too vividly how unhappy he had been when she left England and knew that he would not see her again.

He had always been a little shy about expressing his feelings like most Englishmen and he confided in no one.

Nevertheless it had often been hard to sleep at night when he thought about Monica.

'I love her and she loves me and it does not matter to her whether I am rich or poor.'

Yet it would make life much easier in the future as he would be so rich.

It was tremendously satisfying to know that Monica had loved him for himself when he was poor.

Georgie was certain that Sir Desmond, who was an extremely clever man would have known when he saw the London House closed and Ranmore Park dilapidated what the position was.

Now everything had changed.

'Just how can I have been so incredibly lucky?' he asked himself again and again before he fell asleep.

CHAPTER SEVEN

On Sunday night at Sandringham there were only two neighbours invited to dinner as it was a quiet evening.

The Prince, as he did not gamble on a Sunday, said when he joined the ladies that he would play bridge.

The Princess then countered with her own idea.

"I thought out a new way of playing hide-and-seek. One of the ladies will hide and the others will look for her. When each person finds her, they will stay with her until the whole party has found her. There will be a prize for the first person and a consolation for the last."

They all laughed at her idea and agreed it would be fun to play it.

"I am going to ask Miss Ellie-May to be the first to hide, because she will not know the house as well as some of you – and that will mean that she will doubtless find an original place which none of us have thought of before."

"Oh, I do hope I can do that," cried Ellie-May, "and it's such a lovely idea."

Galina realised that she was thrilled with the idea of exploring Sandringham.

"We will give you exactly ten minutes from now," said the Princess, "then we will come to search for you."

Ellie-May gave a jump of delight and hurried away.

The others continued to talk about Bramton Priory and how thrilled they were with their tour of the house.

"I just cannot believe," the Princess enthused, "that anyone could own so many marvellous collections."

"I am very proud of it," replied Lord Bramton, "and as you can understand, ma'am, I do not want to lose it."

"Of course not. We will all think of ways it can be saved."

Galina was thinking that she would tell him on their way home of her idea of opening the Priory to the public.

However, she could not help but think there would have to be an enormous number of visitors to provide the amount of money he needed.

The Princess kept her eye on the clock.

"Now. It is ten minutes to ten and we can all go to hunt for Miss Ellie-May."

Galina had a vague idea of where she might go.

When they had been shown around the house, she had been very interested in a small but well furnished room – in it there was a heavy velvet curtain that could be pulled across the centre of the room.

"Why do you think it is there?" she had asked.

"I cannot imagine, unless His Royal Highness has secret conversations in this room with someone who does not wish to be seen and identified."

She had said that just to be amusing, but Ellie-May had thought it an intriguing idea.

"I have always thought," she sighed, "that spies are very brave. After all, it must be terrifying to think at any moment you might be recognised and exposed."

Galina was aware that Ellie-May enjoyed reading detective stories and therefore agreed with her.

'I am quite sure that is where she will go,' she told herself as they all left the drawing room.

She walked along the twisting corridors and there were a great number until she found the right room.

When she opened the door, the room was in total darkness and she thought she must have been mistaken.

Then as she stood there hesitating, she heard Ellie-May whisper,

"Is that you, Galina?"

"Oh, I have found you!" exclaimed Galina.

She went into the room and closed the door.

"Where are you?"

"By the window."

Galina groped her way across the room.

When she reached the window she found that Ellie-May had pulled back the curtain so that the moonlight was streaming through.

She was sitting by the window and the moonlight haloed her.

She was well hidden behind the velvet curtains and she had pulled them half-way across the room.

"I think you are cheating to hide so cleverly!"

"I was quite certain they would not find me in here, but I guessed you might remember just how intrigued I had been with the 'spy room' as I called it."

Galina sat down beside her.

"I think perhaps we are both cheating because I was more or less reading your thoughts. What I will do is to go back and join the others and then find you later."

"I think that's sensible. We don't want Her Royal Highness to think we are thwarting her game."

"No, of course not."

Galina pulled the curtain open a little bit further and peeped out of the window.

"It is so beautiful out there," she said. "I do feel we should be playing in the moonlight."

Ellie-May laughed.

"That would be easier."

"I suppose so," Galina sighed a little wistfully.

She left Ellie-May and went back into the other part of the house where she could see everyone looking behind sofas, curtains and into cupboards.

But no one had any idea where Ellie-May might be.

Then as she was going up the stairs to the first floor, she met Sir Christopher coming down.

"I can see you have not found Ellie-May," he said.

Galina, not wishing to tell a lie, just smiled at him.

"I have to find her, Galina. Do have you any idea where she is likely to be, because her father wants to speak to her?"

She hesitated for a moment.

"I do not want to spoil Her Royal Highness's new idea of hide-and-seek, but if you look in the room with the velvet curtains across it without being observed, you will be able to tell Ellie-May that she is wanted."

Sir Christopher smiled at her.

"Thank you. It is most kind of you."

He hurried off as someone was now coming up the stairs.

After a while Galina went downstairs and thought she would go to the conservatory, as she wanted to have a last look at the flowers before she returned to London.

On the way she passed the library and noticed that the door was ajar.

She knew that there was a better collection of books here than in any of the other houses she had visited.

On the Princess's orders every room was either in darkness or left with just two or three candles for lighting.

In the library there were just the three candles on the mantelpiece and Galina thought she would take one so that she could read the titles of some of the many books.

She closed the library door and moved through the darkness towards the mantelpiece.

Suddenly someone emerged from the shadows and put his arms round her.

She opened her mouth to give a cry of astonishment and then realised who it was.

"I knew you would come here!"

Without waiting for an answer, Lord Bramton lips came down on hers.

He kissed her wildly and fervently.

It was as if something had broken inside him and he could no longer control himself.

He kissed Galina until she felt as if he was carrying her up into the sky and they were touching the stars.

Then he raised his head and exclaimed,

"It's just no use, my darling, I cannot go on without you."

"I love you so much, Victor," Galina gasped.

"Do you love me enough to risk the future without money and without any help?"

"We will surely find a way of saving ourselves and the Priory – "

"I knew you would say that, my precious one."

Then he was kissing her again.

It seemed a long time before they could speak and then Lord Bramton breathed,

"I thought at dinner when I heard the man next to you paying you compliments and telling you how beautiful you are that I could not stand it any longer.

"I would kill any man who comes near you. I want you more than I have ever wanted anything in my whole life. In fact, if you stopped loving me, I would die!"

"I love you. I adore you," cried Galina. "But I feel that you should marry Ellie-May and save the Priory."

"Not even the Priory itself is as important as you, my darling one. Everything in it is dead, but you and I are alive and what is left of our lives, we must spend together."

Galina gave a small cry of happiness and then he was kissing her again.

Someone pulled open the library door and they both stiffened – at the same time they did not move or speak.

Whoever it was, looked in, saw that the room was in darkness except for the candles and went away.

Lord Bramton drew Galina beside him on the sofa and put his arms round her.

"My darling Galina, my loved one. How soon can we be married."

"Just as soon as Georgie comes back from America, and I would like to marry you in your lovely little Chapel."

Lord Bramton stared at her.

"Do you really mean it?"

"Do you think I would want a big wedding that we cannot afford with lots of people staring at us and saying we are crazy?"

Lord Bramton laughed.

"You are absolutely right and, of course, it would cost money we do not have."

"We must save every penny we can, Victor, and I

have an idea as to how we can make a little money which I will talk to you about tomorrow."

"All I want to do is to kiss you. I have controlled myself for so long it is impossible to go on any longer. I love and worship you – everything about you is so perfect.

"Do you think that Georgie will be very angry with you for not marrying someone rich as he wanted you to?"

"He may be a bit disappointed, but you know how fond he is of you and if he thinks money is so important, he should marry Ellie-May himself!"

"I think Ellie-May has other ideas," Lord Bramton confided, "and so has someone else."

"What do you mean?"

"I have a suspicion that Sir Christopher is falling in love with her. He was talking about her last night and there was a look in his eyes which told me he felt more deeply about her than anyone else."

Galina gave an exclamation.

"I passed Sir Christopher on the stairs and he asked me where Ellie-May was hiding, as he had an important message for her from her father."

"So you told him where she was. Then how did you know?"

"She was in a place that she and I have called the 'spy room' and I felt certain that was where she would be."

"Instead I have found you, my darling."

"I am so glad you found me," she whispered.

Then as he kissed her again, it was just impossible to think of anything but to thrill to the wonder of his lips.

It was a long time later that Lord Bramton said,

"I think really, my lovely one, we ought to go back to the drawing room. I am sure everyone has found Ellie-

May by this time and they will think it rather strange that we are missing."

Galina gave a laugh.

"Does it matter what they think?"

"No, of course not," he answered. "But as you say we must wait until Georgie returns before we announce our engagement. Then we will go to the Priory and have the most wonderful wedding anyone could ever wish for."

"I only hope, Victor, that you will not believe your Greek Goddesses to be more beautiful than me!"

"How could they be? As far as I am concerned you are the *most* beautiful woman in the world and I am the luckiest man to have you as my wife."

He kissed her again.

Hand in hand they walked from the library back to the drawing room.

They were nearly there as she could hear the chatter of voices, and then they could see that Ellie-May and Sir Christopher were coming towards them.

Galina gave a little cry.

"Has no one found you?"

"No one except for Christopher," Ellie-May replied looking up at him.

There was a silence and then Lord Bramton said to Sir Christopher,

"I have a feeling I should be congratulating you."

Sir Christopher laughed.

"Is it that obvious? But of course neither Ellie-May nor I can admit anything until we have asked her father."

Ellie-May looked at Galina.

"We are going to be *married*," she whispered.

Galina put her arms round her and kissed her.

"I am so glad, so very glad, and I know you will be blissfully happy."

"I will make certain of that," said Sir Christopher. "But for Heaven's sake, do not say a word until I have told His Royal Highness, as he always likes to know a secret before anyone else."

"We will be very careful," promised Galina, "and perhaps it would be wise, as no one has found Ellie-May, if I take her in alone and you two men pretend you have been looking for her. Then you can come in later and say you have given up the chase."

"That is a good idea," agreed Sir Christopher.

He started to walk back the way he had come and a little reluctantly Lord Bramton followed him.

Galina waited until they were out of sight and then holding Ellie-May's hand they went back into the drawing room.

"I have found her," she cried, "but she was very well hidden and as it is so late, I have made her come back to civilisation!"

The Princess came towards them.

"That is very sensible of you. Ellie-May, everyone said you had disappeared and we could not imagine where you were clever enough to be hiding."

"I am not going to tell anyone," answered Ellie-May, "because Your Royal Highness may want to play the game again and it must be an undiscovered secret."

The Princess laughed.

"You are right and you must have a special present for being so clever. Are we all here?"

As she spoke the door opened and Sir Christopher looked in.

"Oh, there you are Miss Ellie-May!" he exclaimed with surprise. "I was very worried when I heard so many had given up that I was just going to send for the Police."

"Oh, don't do that! I might well be charged with something I have not done."

"You will certainly not be charged with anything," said the Princess, "and I think everyone deserves a glass of champagne after their arduous efforts to find you. You are the first who has ever succeeded in remaining completely hidden and I think it is very ingenious of you."

It was impossible for Ellie-May to say anything.

Although some guests pressed her to tell where she was hiding, she shook her head.

"I am the first person," she boasted finally, "to have left a secret at Sandringham!"

*

The next morning when they left in the train Galina was not surprised that Sir Christopher went with them.

After they said goodbye to the Prince and Princess, she heard the Prince saying to him,

"Don't be too long in London. I shall miss you."

"I will be back here as soon as I can, Your Royal Highness."

When they got into the Royal Compartment, Ellie-May sat down next to Sir Christopher.

Galina then sat as far away as possible beside Lord Bramton.

"Have you slept well, my darling?" he asked in a low voice that no one else could hear.

"I was too happy to sleep for long – "

"I felt the same and I feel today as if the sunshine has never shone so brightly and the birds have never sung so beautifully."

"It is so wonderful to be with you," sighed Galina.

The train started off and Mr. Farlow, who had been generously tipping all the porters, moved further into the compartment.

Then to Galina's considerable surprise he came and sat down beside them.

"I want to talk to you, Victor," he began.

"And I have something to say to you, sir," replied Lord Bramton. "But of course you speak first."

"Very well, I have been cogitating all night about your amazing collection at the Priory and I have realised it is, in fact, exactly what I want for myself in America."

Galina thought he was going to ask if he could buy some of it and she felt it would be uncomfortable for Lord Bramton to have to explain the difficulties of entailment.

But before she could speak, Mr. Farlow went on,

"I know it's all entailed and that it's impossible for you to sell anything to me, even one small piece of ivory."

"That is the truth, sir," nodded Lord Bramton.

"Well, what I'm going to suggest is that, as you are so knowledgeable, you will buy for me from all over the world, a collection of antique pieces as closely resembling your own as it is possible to find."

Galina gave a little gasp.

"If you will agree, I will give you the sum of ten thousand pounds a year for your trouble until the collection is complete and, of course, all your expenses will be paid down to the last dime."

It was obviously with difficulty that Lord Bramton found his voice.

"If you really mean it, sir, I can only say that it is the most superb idea I have ever heard. I only hope I will not fail to find you antiques which, if not exactly like mine, are unusual and precious."

It was then that Galina gave a little cry.

"How could you think of anything so marvellous? I know there is nothing he would enjoy more than finding you what you require. Also if you can give Victor all that money, we can be married at once and I will be able to go with him."

Mr. Farlow smiled.

"I thought that was what you would say and I can only wish you both much happiness."

"I am lost for words," sighed Lord Bramton. "I can only thank you, sir, from the bottom of my heart and I will strive in every way to find what you desire. Although it will take time – the sort of pieces you require are available, if one looks for them in the right places."

"I believe your experience would know where those places are and I intend to be envied by every householder in Fifth Avenue when I come up with a treasure which not one of them has the slightest chance of owning!"

He was obviously so overjoyed at the idea that both Galina and Lord Bramton laughed.

"I promise you I will make you not only the envy of New York but of the whole American Continent!"

"That is exactly what I want, and thank goodness I can afford it!"

He rose from his seat as he spoke and added,

"I think I should tell Ellie-May what we have now agreed, otherwise she might feel out of it."

Galina knew that Ellie-May had yet to tell him *her* secret, so she did not say anything.

Mr. Farlow made his way across the compartment and sat down beside his daughter.

Galina slipped her hand into Lord Bramton's.

"I am dazed, Galina, as I thought last night when I kissed you and you said that you would marry me, I had touched the moon and could ask for nothing else. But now Mr. Farlow has given me the stars as well and I cannot find words with which to thank him."

"I think it is bright of him to think of it. He knows that, if you can give him what he wants, he will be the envy of his friends and the most talked about millionaire in the whole of New York."

"I thought he was that already with his oil wells!"

*

They had nearly reached London before Mr. Farlow left the seat next to Ellie-May and he came back to where he had been sitting with Galina and Lord Bramton.

"I suppose you will have guessed what Ellie-May has been telling me?"

"She is incredibly happy," replied Galina. "And it was impossible to keep it a secret."

"Well, he's surely a nice enough fellow, although to be honest, I don't mind telling you I would have liked an Earl or a Duke for my daughter."

There was silence before Lord Bramton remarked,

"I think actually she has done better than that."

"How do you mean!" Mr. Farlow asked sharply.

"Well, as you already know Christopher's mother is a relative of Princess Alexandra. It means Ellie-May will be welcome at Sandringham or Marlborough House. There will be no question of her not being invited to every party given by Their Royal Highnesses and she will be received by Queen Victoria at Windsor Castle."

It was obvious that Mr. Farlow had not thought of this and he commented happily,

"If that's true, it's *very* satisfactory indeed!"

"Of course it is true, and I know, as she is so pretty, she will undoubtedly become, in time, one of the important hostesses in the whole of London."

Mr. Farlow gave a deep sigh.

He had merely thought Sir Christopher's Baronetcy was rather low down on the Social scale.

"Frankly," Lord Bramton finished, "I do think that Ellie-May's marriage will be the most illustrious wedding of the Season. I can promise you everyone will want to be there and there will be crying and weeping from those who do not receive an invitation!"

Mr. Farlow looked even more delighted.

"We can hold the reception at Ranmore House and the ballroom will be about big enough."

"I would hope so," came in Galina. "But if it is not and too many accept your invitation, you can always erect a really big marquee in the garden behind the house."

"Yes, of course we can. I'd not thought of that."

He was obviously thrilled with the idea and then he asked,

"I suppose Sir Christopher, my future son-in-law, will have a very large number of guests, who will expect to be invited."

"He has a most extensive family," answered Lord Bramton, "and as he was educated at Eton and served in the Household Cavalry, I should imagine that his friends run into thousands, not counting the Social world, who will expect to be invited as it will be such a smart wedding."

By the time they reached London, Mr. Farlow was smiling with satisfaction and he was already thinking how envious his friends and enemies in America would be.

Just before they actually drew up on the platform, Lord Bramton suggested,

"There is one thing I know that will make you very happy and that is your daughter is not being married for her money."

Mr. Farlow looked at him enquiringly.

"Sir Christopher's father was a very rich man and I know that Christopher has always had more money than he needs. You will certainly be impressed with his house in Oxfordshire which is almost the size of Sandringham. He also has a house in Berkley Square which has been in the family for several generations."

Galina put her hand into his and said very softly,

"Ellie-May is marrying Sir Christopher because she loves him and he is marrying her because he has lost his heart."

"That's exactly what I wanted for her."

Galina knew there was a note of relief in his voice.

They were all driven to Ranmore House and when luncheon was over, Lord Bramton said he was going out.

"Where are you going?" Galina enquired.

"I am going to see a good friend of mine who is the curator at the Tate Gallery."

"To ask his advice?"

"Yes, and I am going to consult the experts at both Sotheby's and Christie's. Quite a number of objects I wish to collect automatically come up at their sales, but I think you realise, my darling, we will be spending quite a lot of time abroad."

"It will be more exciting than anything else, Victor, to go abroad with you and see the places I have only been able to read about."

"We will explore them all together and it just seems incredible that we can do it in such comfort and spend what money we please in finding precious objects to make Mr. Farlow even more envied than he is for his oil wells!"

"That is true and I do think we are really doing the right thing not only for him but for America itself."

He knew exactly what she was saying and nodded,

"As they are a young nation they need the old and it is vitally important that the objects of the old world should enrich the new."

"I knew you would think like that. So we are really on what is almost a holy mission – "

"That is how I want you to think of it, because you are going to work as hard as I am. But there is one issue that is more important than anything else."

"What is that, Victor?"

"We must not fail as we both realise we are not just spending a rich man's money, but are bringing education, inspiration and perhaps ambition to the young people of a new and great country."

Galina threw her arms round his neck.

"I love you! I love you!" she cried. "You always say the right words and even if we have to be as poor as I thought we would be, I know you would still have gone on thinking in the same way."

"It would have been more difficult – "

"But I still think that after what you have said, we should let people visit the Priory to delight their minds and educate their brains with your wonderful possessions."

Lord Bramton stared at her.

"I never thought of that."

"You must think it over very carefully, Victor, but I

think it is wrong for your amazing collections to have been shut away for so long, and to have only been visited in a surreptitious way by those brave enough or perhaps cheeky enough to bribe your servants."

She saw that he was listening and went on,

"Surely it is important that the people of England should find out all about great houses and for the young to learn an easy history lesson that is not in a book."

"You are quite right, of course, you are quite right, my darling Galina."

He drew a deep breath.

"What we will do is to put our own house in order as soon as we are married. We will put reliable servants in charge so that when we are not there, visitors can see our treasures, but not try to steal them."

"I am sure it is only a case of organisation."

"It was your idea, Galina, and therefore I will leave it to you. I am now going off to talk with the Curators of museums and picture galleries. Then as soon as we can, we will start our trips abroad."

Galina flung her arms round Lord Bramton's neck.

"I love you, Victor, I adore you. And what is most exciting is that we can do all these things together."

"It is what I have been wanting all my life, although I did not realise it. Now my precious, beautiful one, I have the greatest treasure of them all and that is you. Only I am far too selfish to even think of sharing you with anyone. I want you completely and absolutely to *myself*."

Galina giggled.

"That is exactly what you are going to have," she sighed as his lips held her captive again.

*

There was so much to think about and so much to do.

With two weddings to be planned, Galina admitted later she was not as worried as she should have been about Georgie.

She had received his telegram a week or so ago that he was coming home.

She thought he would be surprised and delighted at Mr. Farlow's and Lord Bramton's plans.

Then just before he was due to arrive, she began to worry.

Would Georgie be very hurt at her leaving him?

And how would he manage alone in Ranmore Park after Mr. Farlow had gone back to America and they had closed up the house in Park Lane?

One of the problems, however, was solved the night before Georgie returned.

"I am hoping, Galina," said Mr. Farlow, "that you and your brother will allow me to go on living here when I visit London, which, as you realise, will be very frequently once Ellie-May is married."

"Would you be prepared," Galina asked him a little nervously, "to allow Georgie to keep on the servants? You know he cannot afford to pay for them."

"Everything will be exactly as it is now, and if you and your new husband are gallivanting over the Continent, I think perhaps Georgie will be quite happy to have me as a companion if there is no one else."

"Of course, he will," Galina enthused, "and thank you very much for saying you will keep the house going."

"I am still waiting to see your house in the country. Victor tells me that the pictures are even better than any of his."

"He is quite right, but we don't have so many other pieces of art as Victor owns."

They were all waiting eagerly for Georgie's return when the day finally came.

As he was travelling overnight in the sleeper from Liverpool, Galina said there was no point in them all going to the station to meet him.

She knew he disliked a fuss in the early morning.

"I will just take a carriage and two servants to see to his luggage."

She was in fact being extra fussy, as she was afraid Georgie might be upset at her engagement and criticise the arrangements she had made with Mr. Farlow.

So much had happened since he had gone away.

She began to think how difficult it would be to start from the very beginning and explain to him everything that had happened since he had been in America.

She was definitely nervous and kept glancing at the clock before he arrived.

Lord Bramton put his arm round her.

"You are not to worry, my darling, I know Georgie will be delighted with everything you have to tell him."

"I am so frightened that he will be lonely and even though I do indeed love my brother, I find it impossible at the moment to think of anyone but you," she whispered.

She saw by the expression of love in his eyes that there was really no need to tell him so.

"All I really want is for Georgie to hurry up so that he can be Best Man at our wedding."

They had already arranged for the ceremony to take place early next week.

"I have already waited an agonising year for you," said Lord Bramton, "and I will have a nervous breakdown if I have to wait any longer!"

Galina too had no wish to wait any longer either.

When she heard Georgie's voice coming from the platform, she ran forward and flung her arms around him.

"*You are back*! You really are here. It seems like a century since you went away!"

"I am home," answered Georgie, "with so much to tell you I don't know where to begin."

Galina gave a laugh.

"That is just what we have been saying. Have you had breakfast?"

"Yes, I had it on the train."

He then saw Lord Bramton standing beside her.

"I am so pleased to see you, Victor. How are you?"

"Very very happy."

The way he spoke made Georgie glance from one to the other.

"What has happened?" he enquired.

"Our world has been turned upside down," Galina exploded, "and we want to tell you all about it."

They drove back to Ranmore House as quickly as they could.

They went into the morning room and were alone.

Galina had insisted firmly that she wished to be the first to tell her brother the news. Ellie-May and her father could come in an hour or so later and they had understood.

Now Galina addressed her brother,

"If you are certain you do not want anything to eat, close the door and listen to all we have to tell you."

"I am going to speak first," insisted Georgie, "as I am the eldest. You are not going to believe it, but it is the most thrilling thing that could ever have happened to me!"

Galina looked at him in surprise.

"The first point is that I have become the partner of a Mr. Wilbur and we have already discovered an enormous oil well in Pennsylvania that is going to bring us thousands and thousands of dollars!"

Galina stared at him in amazement and then Lord Bramton burst out,

"That is marvellous news, Georgie."

"I have not yet finished. We are involved in a great number of developments which I will tell you about later, but it includes telephones and typewriters!"

He realised that they were listening spellbound.

"Next and this is very exciting," he continued, "I am going to marry someone I have loved for a long time, but thought I could never afford it."

"*Married*!" exclaimed Galina.

"I don't think you have met her, Galina, but I know that you will love her. She is the daughter of Sir Desmond Wilcourt, who has been our Consul in New York."

"You are to be married! Oh, how wonderful. I do hope you will be very happy."

"I am only afraid it might upset you, Galina."

"Actually I am being married too!"

Georgie stiffened as he looked at Lord Bramton and exclaimed,

"To Victor! I might have guessed it."

"I just hope that you will approve and give us your blessing," asked Lord Bramton quietly.

"I cannot imagine anyone I would like to marry my sister more than you, Victor, and now I shall be so rich I can afford it."

"As it happens, I can afford it too!"

They told him rapidly, both speaking at once, what Mr. Farlow had offered them and how exciting it would be to carry out his projects.

"What has on earth has happened? sighed Georgie. "Has the world gone completely mad or are we dreaming all this?"

"It is all true! It is true!" cried Galina, "and it is all because our prayers have been answered. I wonder every night how we can be so lucky, but we are and – oh Georgie – it's *so* wonderful!"

"That is putting it mildly, and I have told Monica to come to luncheon as I want her to celebrate as well."

Galina wiped away a tear.

"I am crying because I am so happy. I thought this would never happen. I was so frightened that if Victor and I were married, you might be lonely."

"I was very scared that you would not get on with Monica, but I know you will and although she will help me to put the Park in order, I need you both to help as well."

"You know we will do all we can. Oh, Georgie, how could we be so amazingly lucky?"

They were all saying the same that night when Sir Christopher, Ellie-May and Mr. Farlow joined them.

They sat round the dining room table as it glittered with gold and silver ornaments.

It was then that Lord Bramton rose to his feet.

"I am going to propose a toast and I want you all to realise how important it is. Let us raise our glasses to two young people called Galina and Georgie who through sheer bravery have managed to sweep away all the poverty and misery which menaced them."

There was a "hear! hear!" from the gentlemen and he went on,

"They have come out glorious and on top of their own world in which they will always shine as brilliantly as they are shining now."

He raised his glass to Galina and Georgie.

When they had drunk the toast, Galina spoke out,

"Thank you, thank you, my darling Victor. Georgie and I love you which is more important than anything else.

"We know that everyone here has prayed for love – and has found it – and we must all never forget that love is priceless as it comes from Heaven itself."

Her voice was very moving as she continued,

"It is love which comes from God and whatever we do in the future it is only possible because He is guiding us as He has guided us already."

As she finished speaking and sat down, there was a murmur of agreement round the table.

Then Galina slipped her hand into Lord Bramton's while Ellie-May was already holding Sir Christopher's.

Georgie put his arm round Monica and said quietly,

"*Amen*, Galina, to all you have said, and may we never fail in the future from what is expected of us."

Even as he spoke he knew she was right.

Everything they had done and everything they were to do would only be successful if its foundation was Love.